The Time Warp King

A novel by
Martin Klubeck & Alyssa Bishop

*This book is for my children
and grandchildren,*

*may they find the discipline to control their inner
rebel and the courage to share the artist within.*

I believe that rejection is a blessing because it's the universe's way of telling you that there's something better out there.

- Michelle Phan

1

Yup, he did it again.

It seemed to be a habit, he just wasn't sure if it was really a "bad" habit or not. Most of his classmates would say getting on the Cooper brothers' hit list was bad.

These two had been left back enough times in grade school that they were now at least two years older than everyone else in their grade. The movement against bullying didn't seem to slow these two down.

Leo couldn't help but think of them as Tweedle Dumb and Tweedle Dumber.

Well, he knew they weren't actually dumb. They weren't book smart or even clever, but they weren't actually dumb. If they were dumb, they'd have been kicked out of school a long time ago for going too far. No, they knew how much they could get away with and they pushed it right to the edge.

They were also mean. It would be different if they were mad at the world, upset about their plight – broken home or bad parents...but they actually had a pretty good life.

They walked around with an air of entitlement. Like everyone owed them something, and regardless if you agreed or not, they were going to take it from you.

Nope, they were just mean.

Leo kept looking for a reason to cut them some slack, but couldn't find one.

They picked on pretty much everyone, including Leo,

and that he could let pass. But on occasion they went too far. Not far enough for criminal prosecution, but too far, in Leo's opinion, to let it slide.

And today was one of those occasions.

Their victim today was Jeremiah Wilkins. They were teaming up on Jeremiah who was at best 40 pounds and a good foot smaller than either of them. Leo didn't know what had set the brothers off, but it didn't matter.

He was leaving after the last bell and saw the crowd by the bleachers. Far from the bus lines (too many teachers and bus drivers there) and the pickup lanes. This was supposed to be a private affair – only bullies, victims, and spectators.

He knew he should just go on his way. He had his own troubles.

He had finally gotten up the nerve (it took him three weeks) to ask Ellie Joyce out, and she had said she'd let him know. His grandfather was in the hospital. He didn't have transportation, so if he missed his bus he'd have a long walk home.

He knew he should just get on the bus.

"It's the Coopers! They're going to hurt that new kid" someone said as they rushed by him toward the crowd.

That bothered him.

It wasn't that the Coopers were going to do their thing to some new kid in town. Or that the Coopers would humiliate the kid (isn't it bad enough not having any friends, being in a new town, being alone?). Or even that anyone from the school who should stop it, wouldn't get there until after the crowd noise got loud enough to signal they were too late.

None of that convinced Leo to add his name to the Coopers' hit list.

What pushed him over the edge was the way the hopeful spectator had said, "They're going to hurt that new kid." It was only a breathless whisper, but he had heard glee and excitement in that voice.

It wasn't bad enough that they were bullying the new kid, but the same idiots that were being bullied last year (or last week) by the Tweedle Brothers were actually going to enjoy seeing someone else get the same treatment.

For the life of him, Leo could not figure this out.

And it was this confusion, this ridiculous acceptance of what was so clearly wrong, that pushed him to act.

He walked quickly and purposefully towards the crowd. It wouldn't do to get there late, then he'd be one of the spectators.

He pushed his way through the circles. The outer ring was the smallest of the spectators, freshmen and some eighth graders who had come over from the junior high. The next ring was a general mix of curious gawkers. Finally the inner ring, which actually resisted his pushing through, was made up of bully-wannabees. The ones who took it upon themselves to keep the masses from rising up against the Coopers. As if they might all come brandishing pitchforks and torches. In reality, no one in that crowd would ever think to band together to stop the show. They might be secretly (for a few brave souls, even publicly) happy if the Coopers went too far and got expelled. They might even wish that they'd go so far that they ended up in prison. But no one would actually lift a finger or even a voice to stop them.

Usually the inner circle just had to keep the crowd from closing in too far. They didn't expect anyone to actually try to enter the ring!

When Leo got there he didn't hesitate. He slipped easily into the open space and quickly surveyed the situation. The larger Cooper was holding Jeremiah up by his backpack. He was actually holding the kid up off the ground with one large hand. He had locked his elbow next to his side so he could hold the kid without tiring. If the kid had flailed around, he would likely have landed a heel to Tweedle Dumber's groin, but he instinctively knew better. He hung there limply, quietly, waiting for the ordeal to end.

Even Jeremiah knew that the Coopers couldn't go "too" far, could they?

The shorter Cooper (who was as tall as Leo and a lot thicker) was starting to pull down Jeremiah's pants. Before he could finish Leo came up behind him and smacked him in the back of his head. He did it with as much flair as he could. It was a move he'd seen the football coach do to the Offensive Linemen when they made a mistake. Of course they were wearing helmets at the time. Tweedle Dumb wasn't.

The smack made a resounding and satisfying loud clap.

Tweedle Dumb let go of the kid's pants and started to wheel on his assailant. He only got a "Wha…" out, before Leo Placed his foot on that sizable butt and pushed forward with all of his weight. It wasn't a kick, that wouldn't do what he wanted. Instead Leo shoved him while he was starting to turn, his balance totally off. The shove sent him flying forward.

Tweedle Dumb took two stumbling, baby steps forward, trying to regain his balance. It wasn't going to happen.

Tweedle Dumber's reflexes weren't half bad. He never saw Leo, not even after the smack or the kick (his brother blocked the view). But he *heard* the smack (everyone for three blocks did) and he saw his brother stumbling forward. He yanked Jeremiah to the side so his brother's face didn't end up in the kid's crotch.

Nice reflexes.

Instead Tweedle Dumb's hands flailed at the air, found nothing to grab hold of, and he finished falling forward. The crown of his head went full force into Tweedle Dumber's crotch instead.

The rest happened quickly.

Tweedle Dumber dropped the kid, tried to keep from falling backwards, and ended up grabbing his brother's shoulders. They both went down, backwards, hard. It got worse because with the sound of the smack and the entrance of a new player in the game, the crowd started surging forward. Of course the inner circle tried to hold them back, which kept them from noticing the Cooper brothers tumbling into them.

The melee became a mound of falling bodies, with the Tweedles at the bottom of the pile.

A loud cheer erupted from behind Leo. He knew they weren't cheering for the Coopers getting a taste of their own poison. They were cheering because something, anything, had happened. Perhaps they wouldn't have cheered as loud if the Coopers had succeeded?

Jeremiah straightened up his belt – most kids don't wear them, but his had saved him. He double-timed it to his bus, making it just before the doors closed.

Leo also didn't wait around for round two. But he didn't leave as quickly.

He walked away at his normal pace. Still too angry to be scared.

With the noise level rising, the adults finally made their way toward the bleachers. They passed Leo without a word, and he didn't offer one either.

Even at his slower pace, he got lucky and was able to catch his bus too.

He felt a vibration in his pocket. He pulled out his phone and saw there was a text from Ellie.

I like you, but not like that.

He read the text again.

Yup, she had really texted him that classic line.

Wow, how original. He should have known it wasn't going to end well when she said she'd let him know, like she had to check her calendar.

But a text? Really?

He prepped his thumbs. They hovered over the phone.

What would he write, *Thanks?*

He put the phone back in his pocket.

Leo knew he wasn't popular, he was a bit of a loner, but that was by choice. He had found out a long time ago that being popular in high school required a personality he didn't have.

A personality flaw really.

Leo was too nice. His grandmother would say *compassionate.*

He got off at his stop and ran across Cedar Street, hitting the gap in the mild traffic with room to spare.

This time his phone vibrated at a quicker tempo, meaning he had a call coming in.

The only person he knew who ever actually used a cell phone to talk was his Grandmother.

"Yes Grans?" he answered.

"Are you going to be home for dinner?"

"Sure. I'm just stopping by the library" he said as he reached the double doors. He didn't go inside yet.

"Ok, dinner will be at 6, rain or shine," she said and hung up.

Leo once again put his phone in his pocket and hit the handicap door opener for the library. He was inherently a rule-follower. He had never seen the inside of detention, got good grades, and was actually one of the local teenagers who were greeted with a smile by adults.

That's why he put his phone away before entering the library (using cell phones was not allowed). But his minor rebellious act of using the automatic door opener wasn't an act of disobedience. It didn't say it was restricted for handicap use only – like the three parking spots closest to the entrance. And he loved how it felt to make the doors swing wide with the touch of a button.

"Hi Mrs. Hunsberger," he said to the librarian working the circulation desk.

"Hi Leo," she answered.

He smiled at her.

Mrs. Hunsberger liked Leo. Most people did. She found him to be well spoken, polite, and respectful. She also thought he was a rather handsome teenager. Not like the football jocks (they never came to the library anyway), and not like one of those boy-band singers. He had a very pleasant face to go with his demeanor and he always gave her a smile. She liked that.

She wished more young people would smile. They all seemed so serious.

"What are you looking for today? How about something cheerful?" she asked.

She knew why he had become a regular customer. He wasn't normally a big reader. But ever since his grandfather had become seriously ill, he had been getting books out to read to him.

"I'm thinking maybe action," he said.

For the last six months his grandfather had been in and out of the hospital. Mostly in.

"Old-school or something new?" she asked.

"Jack Reacher or Jack Ryan, no fantasy" he said. He didn't want to deal with any more fantasies. Between his thinking Ellie Joyce could like him like that, and his grandfather's drug-induced imaginings, he figured he needed a break.

"Let's see what we can find." She started searching the library's online catalog.

He settled on one of the earlier Reacher novels.

Now for dinner and then a late night visit to the hospital. Luckily everything was in walking distance. He still had two more lessons to go for Drivers' Ed class, and his grandmother didn't drive.

He thought, not for the first time, that this wasn't fair. Most of his classmates were getting ready for the summer, anticipating fun and freedom from school. Their last summer before their senior year. The last chance to have fun before thinking more seriously about college or work.

Who are you fooling? He thought.

He had thought and worried over his future since he entered high school. But after this summer he'd have to make a decision. He was not looking forward to the craziness of the coming senior year.

Worse though, was that his grandparents needed him. He couldn't go traveling this summer like one of his friends. He couldn't take an internship in Chicago or New York. He couldn't go anywhere or do much of anything but stay put.

His grandfather, the man who had raised him for the last ten years, was dying and that made it his turn to step up. They had stepped up when his parents died. They raised him when they should have been enjoying their retirement. Now it was his turn to help them.

On his walk home, he decided what he'd tell Ellie. He took out his phone and texted her a short reply.

No worries, he texted.

And he meant it.

It takes a unique personality to lead. And even if you have the makings of a King, you may not have the desire.

- Young Phillip

2

"I let my country and my people down," Leonard Hardy whispered. His already pale face fading another notch into ghostly white. Like a chameleon, he was slowly blending in with the sterile white of the hospital room. Like a trapped, dying chameleon.

Two days ago they moved him from a shared room where a plastic curtain separated him from another ailing man, to a private room. A dying room. The hospital staff had some quaint name for the room, something like "hospitality suite" or "meditation room." To Leonard it was simply a dying room.

There were lots of yellow and red flowers in vases. Sprigs of green and large purple Iris' jutted out at odd angles. Pots of plants and get-well cards littered every available horizontal space. These splashes of color stood out in the otherwise white room. The only reprieve Leonard had from the sympathy items was the set of large (safety glass) windows which filled the wall to his right. Leonard spent most of his free time staring out those windows. Thankfully they afforded an unobstructed view of the sky. He didn't want to see the small town he lived in. He didn't want to see the streets with cars moving about – people living their lives in sweet ignorant bliss of the pains of others.

It didn't bother him that he was pushed into a quiet room so that no one had to be reminded of his passing.

Leonard Hardy didn't want to be a burden to anyone.

Not to his wife Genevieve or his grandson Leo. Not to the Knights of Columbus, his parish, or his friends. But, seeing everyone going about their daily lives made him feel a little twinge of jealousy. He didn't like being useless, and more importantly (to him) he disliked being a burden to others. He hated that he caused others to waste time.

But Leonard knew these negative thoughts were a waste of *his* time. So he was determined to stop having them.

"I let my country and my people down," he whispered again. Positive thinking was easier said than done.

He wondered, not for the first time, why they hadn't bothered to paint a little color into the walls. If they really wanted to make it more relaxing, they would paint the stupid walls something other than white. He wondered why they couldn't put up a few strategically placed pictures. He figured it was easier to play it safe – blank white walls ran zero risk of offending anyone.

To the right of the bed, between the window and Leonard, was a cushioned rocking chair, occupied by his grandson Leo, and a small night table. Genevieve had removed the white chair and brought in his oak one from home, trying to make him feel comfortable.

Next to the table, slightly behind the rocker was a floor lamp. He liked the floor lamp. It was just a tall pole with a cone on top. The cone opened toward the ceiling, and a large bulb shone light upward, filling the room with a soft light. The overhead fluorescents were still in place, but they were kept off - unless the doctor needed to examine him. If he didn't look at the flowers or the high-tech medical equipment behind, above, and to his left, he could almost imagine he wasn't in a hospital room. Except for the IV bottle hanging next to the bed (and its incessant dripping), the heart monitor's slow, rhythmic beeping, the cold rails on the bed, and the white walls, Leonard could almost feel that the room was actually pleasant.

"I let my country and my people down," Leonard repeated, a little more loudly, while staring out the windows.

His grandson, Leo, continued flipping through a People magazine. *Why didn't they have anything good to read in hospitals?*

He didn't look up to reply.

"You served in World War II and received lots of medals, Grandpa." Leo was bored of this ritual, but he knew it might be one of the last times he'd have to humor his grandfather. It wasn't that he didn't love his grandfather. Actually it was just the opposite. He loved the old dying man so much that sitting and watching him slowly fade away was tearing him apart. But Leo didn't know how to deal with it all and at only sixteen he thought he shouldn't have to.

He had nothing but problems.

Two cretins were trying to bully him because they thought he wasn't cool enough. The girl he had a thing for didn't like him the same way. His teachers felt he was slacking, "you have sooo much potential." His basketball coach actually used the same words.

School sucked.

Grandpa wheezed out a laugh.

Add to that his parents dying over ten years ago and now his grandfather was going to leave him too.

Life sucked.

Grandpa's laugh became a cough.

Leo could tell he was struggling not to lapse into a coughing fit.

Death sucked worse.

Leo stood up smoothly, even gracefully, and took the

glass of water off the night table and held it out. He deftly tilted the straw with two fingers while firmly holding the glass.

"Drink?" Leo asked.

His grandfather sipped the water then laid back onto the overly large pillows, sighing.

"Silly boy. Not here, not *this* country. I mean my home, my *real* home."

Leo had forgotten that his grandfather had been bemoaning his fantasy life. The doctor had warned Leo that his grandfather's mind might slip as the time grew closer, but he knew this wasn't due to him dying – he had been telling *this* story, bits of it anyway, Leo's whole life.

Leo moved the rocker so that he was fully facing his grandfather. He thought he should at least feign interest.

"Sure, Gramps," he tried not to let his feelings show. He looked down at the magazine in his left hand, and decided to put it on the small ledge at the bottom of the night table. He looked at the Jack Reacher novel with the library due date slip sticking out. Perhaps he could just read the book to him.

Maybe if he avoided eye contact he'd be spared. He reached for the book.

No such luck.

"You don't believe me," he hacked out, coughing and taking another sip of the water Leo offered.

"Sure I do, Gramps," he tried not to smile. He didn't want to encourage him. "You're king of a whole other world, which you ran away from, and as your only living descendent, I will be the next king of NASA." Leo announced this litany with as little emotion as possible.

"Nahasar! Leo, honestly, I'm dying here. Try a little won't you?"

With a sigh Leo looked his grandfather in the eye.

"Sorry." He leaned back in the chair. There would

be no Reacher busting heads tonight.

"You just wait. You'll see!" His grandfather said with no anger or malice.

"Funny, I just went in for a checkup, and the doctor said I *see* fine." Leo put an extra-large, 'everything is fine' grin on his face. He wondered if he looked as silly as he felt.

"Leo, you make too many jokes. If only your father were still alive, he'd whip you into shape."

It was a conversation they'd had many times, in many forms. The battle was to see who missed his father more. Leo wasn't ready to think about marriage, fatherhood, or for that matter dying. But, some things are forced upon a person before their proper time. High School was tough enough. His life was a mess and instead of doing what all of his classmates were doing, he was sitting beside his grandfather's hospital bed. What his grandparents and he knew would be a deathbed.

"If my father were alive, you'd be telling *him* this fantasy."

Leo saw the flash of pain flit across his grandfather's face and immediately regretted what he said.

"I'm sorry Gramps."

Not for the first time he wanted to cry out, *why me*, but his grandfather's influence wouldn't let him. Even when his parents died, his grandfather was strong. There was no hesitation – although taking in their six-year old grandson meant starting all over again. When they should have been enjoying their retirement years, the twilight years, Leonard and Genevieve Hardy went about raising their only grandchild as if he were their own.

Leonard took over the work Leo's father had started, the task of making Leo a man. And while Leo didn't buy the whole 'lost world' stuff, he was a good student and easily accepted the values and morals his grandfather taught him.

"It's not a fantasy, boy. You *will* be king."

By the look in Grandpa's eyes Leo knew he wasn't going to stop. He settled in for a long story. When he was little he actually believed it all, and then as he got older, he thought it was quaint, but now, he just found it sad. Leo's loving grandfather, a great guy, a war hero, was just a little off his rocker. He wondered if the story would change, get more outlandish as his grandfather's mind started slipping. But what he found was that he had never heard the whole story. Perhaps his grandfather never thought it necessary before.

Wormholes, in theory, can create a tunnel from one time-space instance to another time-space instance without regard for the current constraints we have put on the structure of our universe. A time machine, in essence, is not a construct as we normally view it, but a means of forming a limited manipulation of space and time, a worm hole that allows travel in a different aspect of our existence. This is in keeping with the geniuses of our time, including Einstein, Newton, and myself. The logic that time travel is not possible because no one has come back from the future is a non-postulate, since the lack of evidence that something exists is an invalid argument against the possibility of its later creation. Besides, just because there is no evidence, doesn't mean it hasn't happened.

> - From testimony given by B. J. Herbert to the Committee on Space Exploration and Land Grants

3

Leonard Hardy was twenty years old when his life underwent drastic changes. It could be argued that the upheaval created by the shift from the teenage years into young adulthood was to be expected - but the changes Leonard was destined to go through would be far from what anyone could have foreseen.

At twenty, Leonard was content to work his quiet, normal job. It gave him plenty of time to read and research all sorts of interesting things. On this day, Leonard was in the largest room of the Museum of Transportation. It housed the most futuristic specimens and the décor complimented the displays. The high ceilings made the room seem even larger than it was. The illumination combined track lighting and hanging spotlights with a third light source emanating from the translucent flooring. Together this created an overly bright effect, putting even the finest subtle detail into high relief. Besides making everything seem futuristic, it also made it easy for Leonard to locate the smallest speck of dust, dirt or debris.

Each artifact had its own display, cordoned off with ropes suspended by evenly spaced chrome poles. Even the most mundane item garnered an awe-filled "ooh!" or "ahh!" thanks to the lighting. Of course it had to all be kept pristine – the slightest smudge of dust would lessen the effect and destroy the ambiance. That's one of the reasons Leonard loved his job – he knew his purpose. He also knew the importance of the museum to the education of the young and old alike.

"Happiness is a by-product of knowing your importance in the world," his father would say.

He wore his all white uniform with pride. He kept it as clean as he did the museum floor. His white shoes and socks matched the white jumpsuit, making it easy for him to blend in with the displays, maintaining anonymity. He knew people came to see the wonderful items on display, not him – and he liked it that way. He pushed his white cart ahead of him. The white cylinder floated a few inches off the ground, using the latest technology to actually vacuum the floor as it went (rather than pushing air out). At first Leonard didn't know how it worked, but his curiosity made him find out. Luckily, he was able to put it back together after he had dismantled it. His broom worked with the same basic tech, acting as a vacuum, making a dust pan unnecessary.

As usual, he was busy cleaning up Onka soda cans and long sandwich ends left on the floor. He had worked his way methodically through the main room, picking up, dusting, and adjusting as he went. He now finished his circuit next to the Time Portal display. He always thought it funny how people seemed to think it was okay to litter when someone else got paid to clean up after them. It didn't really bother him though, he found it humorous. He also loved his job at the Museum of Transportation because it allowed him to spend time in the other museums after hours. That is, he loved it up until the Elder Five approached him with a proposition.

The Elder Five looked just like you'd think based on their title - five old men with long white beards (a requirement for the job) and calm, stern, judgmental faces. Their long flowing robes hid their aging bodies well. It allowed them to retain an aura of wisdom and power, regardless of their physical condition. With the right robes, even an Elder stricken with back spasms could maintain the appearance of health.

A rumor had spread a few years ago that the Elders had replaced their lower bodies with bionics. While no one had seen under their robes for decades, this was eventually discounted as false.

"It is he," whispered the First. He wore a deep red robe with intricate folds, but no visible seams. He was pointing a long bony finger toward a man kneeling near an empty platform. The platform wasn't really empty, but you couldn't see the display from that distance. On the dais sat a small coin-sized metal ring. Amazing, really, that it had never been lost. It was so small and insignificant looking.

"His name tag *does* say Hardy," said the Second, sounding doubtful. His green robe seemed to shimmer with every movement. None of the elders questioned whether the Second could make out the kneeling man's name tag from that distance - not only was it too far for any of them to see, the man's back was to them. Each knew the Second would be right.

"He's a *janitor*," drawled the Third, loudly enough to make visitors look up from exhibitions and stare at them. His robe was green also, but it was a deep, quiet green. A soothing color.

"Of course the man is a janitor, it says so right on his shirt." The Fourth pointed to Leonard's back, where, as he stated, the word JANITOR was written in large white letters. The Fourth's robe was a simple white. Not an off-white, and not a stark, hurt your eyes white. Just a nice solid white that matched his beard and long flowing hair perfectly.

"Ah, but he holds a scepter and gold sphere of status," the First tried, determined to make the best of things. He *had* been the one to spot him.

"That's a broom and an empty soda can! Put your glasses on, you old fool," snapped the Third. He said this a little softer than his original outburst, but still louder than any of the others.

"Who are you calling old?" the First drew himself up. His face turned a deep red, rivaling his robe.

"Why do rulers use gold spheres as symbols of power? Wouldn't a sword be more appropriate?" the Second asked of no one in particular.

"He was calling *you* old – we all are," the Fourth said to the First without any hint of impatience, "and the gold sphere signifies our world, and it is small enough to fit in the hand, so…"

"Enough," the Fifth commanded. They all fell silent. He walked over to Leonard, leaving the others to huddle in silence, watching.

Leonard tried to ignore the old men. He had noticed them as soon as they had entered the museum. He could always tell when trouble was coming his way. He had fully intended to slip out before they could approach him, but when he saw the tall elder in blue leave the group and start toward him, he couldn't do it. He knew it wasn't fear or some sorcerer's spell, it was just his darn curiosity that had kept him from bolting. He lifted the rope and moved out from inside the display area.

"Mr. Hardy? May I have a word with you, Sir?" The Fifth's voice was soft, but demanding. He wasn't surprised to see Hardy hand-stitched over Leonard's right breast pocket.

Leonard deposited his "gold sphere" into his mobile trash container and bowed. He took special care not to clumsily hit the elder with his broom. "Fifth Elder, what may I do for you?"

From across the room the remaining quartet of Elders watched intently.

"Respect," whispered the Second, looking pleased. "And just the right amount of servitude."

The other three elders watched in silence.

"My colleagues and I would like to discuss an important matter. Do you have a moment?" the Fifth said.

Leonard answered by bowing again and sweeping his hand toward the other elders in an "after you" motion. The Fifth bowed back and led him to the group.

No introductions were necessary – everyone knew the Elder Five of Elonce. Each represented one of the five nations, and was greatly respected. Each had a special talent that would have made them important leaders in their own countries, but together they became counselors, sages, and mediators. They were the voice of the Curator.

"You wouldn't happen to be the *head* janitor, would you?" The First asked when Leonard was within earshot.

"Uh, sure. I'm like the king of janitors." Leonard smiled at his own joke. He was the lead janitor in the Museum of Transportation. But then again, he was the only janitor. Each museum had its own staff – three security officers, five researchers, two visitor sponsors, a director, and about ten temporary employees at any given time. But only one janitor.

"King?" asked the Fifth.

"King," echoed the First through the Fourth.

"How amusing," said the Fifth without even the hint of a smile. "Anyway, we're here on official business."

"Official business? For King Harold?" Leonard asked. He guessed it had to do with Nahasar, his home country.

"No, no," the First smiled, showing a great many teeth, "King Leonard Hardy."

The Fifth shot the First a hard glance.

The First was as impatient as the Fifth was patient.

"King Le...heh, heh, heh. Funny, very funny. Is it the Day of Fools already?" Leonard glanced to his left, eyeing the safety of his broom and trash container, over five yards away.

"Not funny, true," said the Second.

"Well, perhaps it is a little funny," said the Fourth, "to think the King of Nahasar is busily cleaning up food scraps in one of the five museums of Elonce. Yes, that definitely qualifies as humorous."

Leonard looked to his right and then back to the left. Although the Elder Five were all standing in a group directly in front of him, he somehow felt surrounded. He half expected a crowd to mob him or a squad of security officers to grab him.

"I'm sorry, but you're next in line, Sire," said the First, not looking sorry at all. In fact, he was beaming.

"We checked with the Oracles," the Fifth began.

"Really?" Leonard asked, stalling for time.

"Three times in fact," the Fifth assured him in his quiet, strong way. "And your line will rule for the next five generations of Hardys." He was trying to sound soothing, and failing miserably. He could see the panic flit across Leonard's face like the shadow of a sparrow, or, maybe it was a sparrow – birds got caught in the museum buildings all the time.

"That will be the longest reign yet," added the Second, trying to be reassuring, but not succeeding.

"I know." Leonard said.

The Third queried, "You knew you'd be king or that your line would rule for 5 generations or that it would be the longest…"

"I knew I'd be king," Leonard said simply.

This took all five by surprise. They hadn't known until just hours before, when King Harold had died unexpectedly. They had been called in immediately. The cause of death still had not been determined, but the question of succession was more important. They had queried the Oracles to find out who the next king of the most important nation on Elonce would be.

"I've known I'm to be king for a while now, it was in a fortune cookie." Then Leonard saw the squad of six security officers, each had the Nahasar seal on their immaculate uniforms and black armbands. They were closing in.

"Fortune cookie? Those are true?" exclaimed the Second. "That means I'll be going on a vacation soon!"

"I'll need my broom…" Leonard said, as he calmly and slowly, backed away from the elders.

"That's not logical," began the Fourth.

"Nor true," said the Third. He signaled for the security guards to move forward.

"Filamental, Elemental, Sincro Senso…" Leonard called out the words as he spun and headed off toward his broom and trash container.

"But Sire, the Oracles are never wrong," said the Fifth

calmly, as the elders walked toward the now running Leonard.

"I know, and neither are fortune cookies." Leonard said. He then called out more strange words. A hum rose up from the floor around the Time Portal display. The small metal coin jumped up and landed on its side. It began to spin. The machine, for that's what it truly was, began to glow a light yellow.

One quick guard beat him to his broom. As Leonard approached, the guard, well trained in royal protocol, bowed deeply.

Leonard took an immediate sharp right turn, slipped under the ropes surrounding the display, and headed straight for the dais. The coin was now expanding and changing shapes. First, a large tube seemed to spurt out of the air above it; then a ring, like a type of sitting furniture, swung out from the far side and continued around to the front until it surrounded the spinning coin. It was spinning so fast now that you couldn't make it out. Then Leonard stepped up on the dais, jumped over the outer portion, and headed toward what must have been the machine's entry point. Two more tubes had emerged from the sides and the spinning ring seemed to wink out and then explode into an enlarged version – over ten feet in diameter. It was a large, round opening which glowed a deep, bright yellow.

"I've spent the last three months researching this thing – and regardless what oracles or cookies say, I'm not going to be king!" He gave a short wave and backed up to the portal opening. The guards got as far as the ropes and stopped. They seemed confused. They were charged with protecting the next king of Nahasar, not capturing him. Also, everyone knew that you were not allowed to go past the display ropes in any of the museums.

The Elder Five pushed past the guards to see the next king of Nahasar sit backwards into the portal as if it were a chair. As he fell through the portal he called out two more sentences and then was gone.

"Should someone follow him?" asked the Second.

The machine gave a high pitched whine and then began to collapse in on itself. It didn't reverse the expansion process, but started to fold down into itself as if it were an intricate piece of origami. Just when it looked as if all the pieces of crunching metal would implode into one chunk of smoking debris, it stopped. Everything stopped. Then began again. It was strange, like time had hiccupped. The coin was back, slowly spinning to a stop, in the center of the dais, seemingly none the worse for the wear.

"No, I guess not," decided the Third.

"What did he say before he disappeared?" asked the First.

"Something about it feeling weird," said the Fourth.

"Yes, and then more nonsense words," said the Fifth.

The First through Fourth looked at the Fifth and nodded. It would not do for anyone else to repeat the "nonsense" words that Leonard had used to activate the portal. They had much to do, very little time to do it, and couldn't afford to have people going on joy rides through time.

"Captain, please post two guards at this display until we return," said the Second to the lead security officer.

"And don't let anyone go past the ropes," added the Third.

"And if King Leonard happens to return, detain him," appended the Fourth.

The Captain looked uncertain, but bowed just the same. The Elder Five headed off toward the exit.

"B-but no one has *ever* used the Time Portal!" gasped

the First, "if that's what it even *is*."

"Of course people have," said the Third angrily.

"They just never return," said the Fourth supporting his argument for action.

"Great, what now?" asked the Second.

"Well unless we can find out how to use the portal, and can find a volunteer to go through it and bring the royal fool back, I suggest we wait," said the Fifth.

"Wait?" asked the First.

"Wait for what?" asked the Second.

"For Leonard Hardy, of course. He *will* rule Nahasar. I don't trust fortune cookies, but the Oracles have never been wrong," said the Fifth.

"So we wait?" asked the First.

"No. Although it has been foretold, we don't know how it shall come to be...so we must do our part," said the Fourth.

"We have much to do," decided the First.

The Second nodded.

"And little time to do it," added the Third.

They all nodded.

"So let's get started," said the Fifth.

"I believe we already have," said the Fourth.

Known as the "war to end all wars," World War One seemed more like a prelude than an end. There was only a 21 year hiatus before the world got back to war. In 1939, the second "World War" began, involving 14 countries across the planet. When it ended six years later, over 47 million people had been killed, with the majority being civilian casualties. It is generally accepted that the war began and ended with the rise and fall of one person. Some believe, no one person should rule a nation.

> - From "The History of War," by J. R. Constable

4

"Gramps?" Leo stood up and leaned over his Grandfather. His grandfather's breathing was steady and deep. He had fallen asleep. Leo pulled the covers up to his chin and kissed him on the forehead. He gathered the juice, cup, and package of Jell-O.

Leo heard his Grandma come into the room.

"He's sleeping," Leo said and left the room quietly, carrying the remnants of the meal. Grandma followed.

"The doctors say he's doing fine," she said.

"He's strong as an ox. He'll be fine." Leo said, but tears were filling his eyes. Leonard Hardy was dying. It was a fact that they'd have to live with soon enough.

"I can't stand seeing him like this," Grans said.

"I know." He put the stuff on the nurses' station and held her hand. "I don't like it either."

"Did he tell you the story about Elonce again?"

"Yes, a little longer story this time though. He even embellished on what happened after he supposedly disappeared – I mean traveled – to our world." Leo couldn't help smiling as he said this. It was such a good story. Maybe someday he'd write a book based on

Gramps' hallucinations. He pressed the down button to call the elevator.

"Want some food? My treat," he offered. They lived within walking distance to the hospital. In some ways this was a blessing, but it also meant Grans never strayed far from her husband's side. Leo figured she could use a break.

"Sure," she said.

They took the elevator to the main floor. Leo couldn't talk his grandma into walking downtown to a restaurant. The cafeteria was as far from her husband as she was willing to go.

They were talking over a pretty awful lunch. In Leo's opinion, hospital food sucked – as a patient or in the cafeteria. He could never figure out why the food tasted so bad.

"What's bothering you Leo?"

"Do you mean besides Gramps dying?" he couldn't help the sarcasm.

"Yes."

He wanted to cry.

Well, Ellie doesn't like me like I like her. The Cooper brothers are probably looking for me so we can have a tag team wrestling match in which I don't have a partner and they don't have to tag in. Coach Deluca says I'm not trying hard enough, and I don't have anyone to share all of this with but my grandma.

What he said was, "I'm fine," and was surprised to realize it was the truth.

She looked at him with a smirk but didn't press him.

"Leo, did I ever tell you how your grandfather and I met?"

"Yes Grans." Unlike the patients' rooms, the rest of the hospital sported a creative design, like a castle. There were two round brick rotundas, which housed meeting places, the rehab room, three lounges, two employee break rooms, and the cafeteria. Unfortunately, very little time was spent on the selection of furniture – the chairs were modern, bright colored, hard, one-piece, and totally uncomfortable. The tables were round, also colorful, and just a tad bit too low to go with the chairs. Or maybe the chairs were too tall. Either way, they had to constantly avoid banging their knees on the underside of the table.

"You two met when Grandpa was hospitalized during World War II. It was when he earned his second Purple Heart for being wounded in battle." Leo took a bite of his sandwich and quickly washed it down with some orange juice. If he was fast enough he might not taste the chicken salad.

"Did I ever tell you why I was at the hospital?" The irony struck him – their relationship started in a hospital, and now, more than likely, it would end in one, too.

"You were a nurse, right?"

"No. I wasn't," she said simply.

When he thought about it, he realized she had never told him she was a nurse. He just assumed it. In fact, he didn't know much about his grandparents and less about his grandfather's time in the war. Leo had seen all the medals and looked at pictures, but he was never sufficiently interested to ask for more details. Grandpa was a great storyteller – but, unfortunately, Leo wasn't much of a listener.

"Why were you there?" He asked.

"I was looking for your grandfather. I had been sent to find him and bring him home."

Great. Now Grans was going senile.

But he knew. He knew, but couldn't believe it. He wasn't one to believe the unbelievable.

"Why? Did all his other brothers die in the war?" Leo heard about them doing that during the war and had seen it in a movie, Saving Private Ryan. He had seen it at his friend's house because his grandparents would never let him watch it – it was way too violent for Grandma and way too realistic for Grandpa. Of course, the "R" rating was the kicker.

He knew he was wrong, but he pressed on anyway.

"Were you one of those special agents that were tasked in finding soldiers that could come home?"

"No."

Leo refused to raise his eyes to look at her.

"I was a special agent, but not that kind. My job was to find your grandfather and bring him back to Elonce."

He looked up. He couldn't believe what he was hearing. He wondered, for a moment, if whatever was affecting Grandpa's mind could be contagious.

They just sat looking at each other.

She was totally serious. When she started to speak again Leo clasped his hands over his ears.

"La, la, la, la, la," Leo sung.

Grans just gave him *the look*.

"Are you going crazy too?" he asked. He was getting angry. "I'm not stupid. You don't have to tell me fairy tales. I know Grandpa is dying."

This time tears welled up in his grandmother's eyes.

"I know," she said.

"Then why are you telling me this?"

"Because you're *not* stupid. Because you know your grandfather is dying. Because it's the truth."

The Elder Five selected three teams of two military agents each, to use the Time Portal and bring back Leonard Hardy. It was Nahasar's number one priority. If the King was not returned and crowned, there would definitely be a civil war. The first son of the late King Harold had a strong group of followers who wanted to make him King, and the head of the Senate wanted the throne for himself. If the chosen king did not take the throne quickly, the two factions would fight over the throne. Only the chosen one would be accepted by each as a rightful successor.

Rather than leave the museum islands, the Elder Five set up shop in the transportation museum. All the information they needed was in the museums anyway. The Elders pulled together a team of the best and brightest minds on the planet – or at least what they could grab at the museums.

After two days of research and selection, the team had all the answers the Elder Five needed to keep the prophecies alive. They walked from museum to museum. The island was a pedestrian campus – no vehicles of any kind were allowed. No roads, no paved walkways, just perfectly cut grass and worn paths. When boats arrived at the docks, visitors even had to turn in their roller blades and personal hovers. This gave the island an interesting contrast – very rustic travel coupled with modern exhibits.

The Time Portal could be programmed using the proper activation words, which one of the historians found in an ancient tome in the Museum of Literature. They could use it safely three times in the small window of time they had. More importantly, they found out how to activate a return gate using a memory cell. The cell was found in the Museum of Energy and was easily duplicated.

Using a projection warp telescope, found in the Museum of Science, they identified three strong instances of Leonard Hardy's DNA signature. It had something to do with a flux factor or a dimensional warp filter. The coincidence was too great to ignore – three safe trips and three strong points in time to visit. It was judged a positive sign by the Elders – all good things come in threes.

The Elders figured out that up to three people could travel through the portal at a time, but they would only send two so that, for the return trip, Leonard would make three. If all went well, at least one team would return with Leonard within a few minutes of being sent, per the return program, and all would be well. At least that was the plan.

Each retrieval team was made up of one female and one male – it was tricky sending anyone on this mission and they decided one of each gender allowed for more contingencies. Not only were they traveling to a different time, it was also to a different world. They couldn't take anything from Elonce besides their clothes, a picture of their target, and the return memory chip, so they didn't adversely affect the history of the world they'd be traveling to. There was a short, but necessary, selection process. Each team was selected from the Museum's Military Linguistic Corps. Each person selected had the talents necessary for the retrieval.

Each was given the opportunity to turn down the assignment.

Of course, no one did.

The teams were given 20 hours of training on the world they were going to – unfortunately, there wasn't much information about Earth in the archives of any of the museums. They were given refreshers on passive restraining methods so they wouldn't hurt the king during collection or transport. They drilled for hours on the words needed to make the memory chip work.

The teams were given garb that would be neutral enough to hopefully fit into any time period, based on what little information they could find.

Both the men and women wore solid color shirts

without buttons. Their trousers were also button-less affairs with drawstrings. Everything was made from natural fibers. Their under-garments and socks were also nondescript. The biggest risk was their shoes. They were all given slip-on canvas shoes with soles made from extra-cured leather. No one thought about inclement weather possibilities on Earth.

Everything was a bit rushed.

When all was ready, the teams drew straws to select which instance they'd be assigned. Everyone wanted to be last, since it would give them the best chance of success. This was logical given the nature of prophecies. Since Leonard Hardy's DNA signature was found in all three time/space locations, it meant that he was there for all three. Chances were high that the first two teams would fail, explaining why the third spike was still on Earth and not in Elonce. But time travel was not an exact science, and no one was sure what could or couldn't be done. If they were looking at history in the form of the spikes, could they actually change anything? Wasn't it already done? This was viewed as a defeatist attitude and therefore set aside. They'd go forward as planned.

The three teams were brought to the Museum of Transportation after closing, on the third night after Leonard Hardy went on vacation (the cover story for his disappearance). They were given their final instructions, a memory return chip (which looked like a small coin of the realm with absolutely no markings), and a pat on the back for luck. The Elder Five worked the machine themselves, calling out the words in a precise and clear manner. The machine jumped to life, hummed loudly and accepted the first two agents. After an hour to allow the portal to cool off, it was activated again, and off went the second team.

Leo must have had his mouth hanging open, because Grans reached over and pushed his chin up.

"Sorry," he said.

"It's okay, Leo. I understand how it must sound."

"But Grans…" he couldn't think of anything else to say, so he didn't. They sat in silence for a while. Finally, Leo pushed his food to the side. He wasn't hungry anymore.

"Let's walk" she offered.

When they left the hospital, they started walking toward the river. It was a beautiful, small town and in the past, they would walk by the river often. The river was about 50 yards at its widest, winding throughout the town. At times it swelled in the rainy season, covering the benches and walkway. Most of the time, like now, the river was calm and quiet, like the town. Most people were at work or in school. It was peaceful.

"Okay. So, you want me to believe that you came to Earth from…some other world?" Leo tried at last.

"And time. Yes." She wasn't going to rush him.

"Hmm." To even consider believing any of it, there were some holes he would need filled.

"Okay Grans, I'm not saying I believe it, but if it is true, what happened to your partner? What happened to the other four agents? How would my going back satisfy the Oracles' prediction?"

"Whoa boy, slow down. One question at a time."

They reached a bench facing the river and sat down.

"Okay. Tell me about your partner, and why you didn't take Gramps back."

"That's still two," she said, feigning anger.

"Okay. Who was your partner?"

"Stan. His name was Stan, and he was a great guy. A

little Gung-ho, but a good guy nonetheless," she started.

"It turned out that your grandfather wasn't as careful with selecting the time as he was with the location for his trip. Earth is very much like Elonce. Some even believe it's a parallel world to ours, and a small group actually thinks it's the same world just so long ago there aren't any records."

"Like the dinosaurs? The only way we know about them is from their fossils. Wouldn't there be stuff like that from us in your world? Couldn't you dig that stuff up?" Leo thought logic might break through his Gran's fantasy.

"Well, we have strict laws about digging and mining – in fact, our laws don't allow for hurting our world in any way, shape, or form. We protect it at all times. Something about our ancestors nearly destroying the planet."

"But, if you could find out what happened, you could stop it from happening again!"

"Dear, when you get back to Elonce, you can argue with the Elder Five to your heart's content. I just know that we don't dig." Leo thought it more likely that he'd end up arguing with someone from social services about not putting his grandmother into a home for the mentally ill.

"Sorry, go on."

"Well, Leonard, bless his soul, picked a pretty messy time to arrive here. The world was in the middle of a war. The United States of America…" she always used the full title – never US, or United States, "…had just joined the war and young, healthy men were needed." They both smiled at that. He had heard some of the stories that went with Grandpa's medals, had heard them repeatedly ever since he was a toddler.

"Your grandfather had run from responsibility, but

not because of fear. He's a very brave man." Leo just nodded and listened. Running away was still running – he wasn't sure he saw a difference.

"After only a week, he enlisted. It was a good thing too – he was having trouble making a living since he only had one set of clothes…"

"And it was a janitor's uniform, right?" Leo added with a smirk.

"Right. The country needed soldiers, and it wasn't too hard to find a recruiting station that would help him enlist, even without any identification or papers. He ended up a war hero and after that he didn't have any troubles finding work."

"Okay, but what happened with you and your partner, Stan?" He was a little proud of himself for remembering the name. This was a more interesting version of the story than he had ever heard before.

"Well, we arrived about five months after your grandfather, but since we were homed in on his DNA signature, we knew he was within a half-mile radius of our landing point. Unfortunately for us, we appeared in the middle of a firefight. Stan was shot, and before I could even duck for cover something exploded behind us, sending us flying through the air. I ended up face down in a muddy foxhole. The next time I saw Stan was in the hospital. He was dead, and the memory recall chip was gone. We had been mistaken for local civilians and been med-evacuated to the nearest military hospital. I had some minor scratches and a nasty concussion.

"It was while I was in the hospital, recuperating, that I found your grandfather. He had been seriously injured saving his squad, which had been ambushed. He ran through a hail of bullets; witnesses claimed that he actually dodged them" at this she smiled, "and took out a machine gun nest. He then took out four more of the enemy before the rest of them ran off."

Leo looked incredulous.

"You don't have to believe me - I'm only telling you what I was told by his squad mates."

"Go on," he said.

"Well, wounded – apparently he hadn't dodged *all* of the bullets – he carried two of his men out of the area, to a safe place where finally he was able to radio for help."

"What, he didn't carry *you* out, too?"

"No. He didn't. I don't even know if he saw us. When the medics showed up with another unit, they made your Grandfather tell them the story, and point out where it had occurred. The officer in charge sent a detail to check it out."

Leo bit his tongue to stop from interrupting.

"Yes, they were the ones who found Stan and me," she answered his unasked question.

"When I saw your grandfather at the hospital, he was peacefully sleeping. I wasn't sure what to do, since I had no way to complete my mission without the chip. I thought maybe I shouldn't let him know who I was; perhaps it would make it harder for the second or third team to succeed if he knew about us. I had just decided to sneak off when he called out to me."

"What did you do?"

"I screamed. Well, not real loud, but he scared me! I thought he was unconscious. He might as well have yelled 'BOO'."

Leo couldn't help laughing.

"Laugh all you want," she said. And she meant it. She wouldn't continue until he got control of himself, which was hard to do. Every time he looked at her, waiting for him to stop laughing, it seemed even funnier.

"Are you done?" She finally asked.

"Yes, I think so." He wiped a tear from his eye, trying

to get hold of himself.

"Well, he must have recognized me because he spoke in our home language. It's a lot like English, but not quite. I had been able to understand the nurses, doctors and other patients if I listened hard and concentrated. But I didn't dare to speak more than a two-word sentence."

"What did he say?"

"Oh, something stupid."

Leo felt more laughter welling up, but he pushed it back down.

"What? Come on. What did he say?"

"He just asked, 'When did they start growing girls as pretty as Elonce women here.' I mean, it was such a corny, stupid line."

Leo couldn't hold it back any longer. He started laughing again. This time she ignored him and went on.

"We talked for hours, until a nurse came and made me go back to my room for the night. I had no friends, no money, nothing. We fell in love, married, and he took me back with him after the war to his new country. I was accepted as a 'refugee wife'. Back then, it was much easier to get into the country and become a citizen."

It took Leo a long time to stop laughing. The big guffaws were over, but he couldn't stop chuckling. He thought part of it might be because he was going crazy too. He realized he was actually starting to believe this fairy tale.

"So, tell me about your life together, about after the war, about Dad." He said.

She just shook her head no.

"That's Leonard's story. He'll have to tell you himself. What I will tell you is about team two, because they aren't going to be able to." It was a custom his grandparents followed - telling a life story. He guessed you shouldn't tell someone else's story, at least not without their permission. Funny, everyone he knew *loved* telling other people's stories as if they were their own.

"Did they die, too?" This was the saddest fantasy he'd ever heard.

"Yes, they did. Please, Leo, listen. I don't think you'll find this part funny." Grans took his hands in hers. Leo sobered up quickly. He knew Grans was right.

"Team two were friends of mine. All of the teams were. Jean and Gary were just young. Too young for their mission. I didn't see them until it was too late. It was the summer that your parents were making their European cross-country trip, celebrating their 10th anniversary. Your mother had planned it for months. She had every stop planned out. Every sight to see, every place to visit, and every moment was on a schedule." They both smiled, deep in their own separate memories.

"We were running late. Your father had forgotten their passports at the hotel - he was like that, and they just made the last call for the train. It was a beautiful locomotive – an old style train. It cost a pretty penny for them to book that trip. An old style train ride across Europe." More smiles.

"Well, they got on, worked their way to a window, and waved goodbye. As the train pulled out, I saw them, Gary and Jean. They were working their way through the cars toward your parents. I almost missed them, because for me, it had been years, and they had dumped the clothes we were issued. They blended in perfectly.

"But Grandpa and you…"

"You have to remember, we were given pictures of Grandpa when he was about your age. And I was a couple of years older than you are now. They didn't recognize us – once they saw your father, they thought they had their man – a little older, but no worse for the wear."

Leo remembered that day, as he remembered it every time he thought of his parents. It was the last time he saw them alive. Grandpa was holding him on his shoulders so he could see over everyone's heads on the platform. A lot of people were waving goodbye to loved ones – unknowingly for the last time.

"Then we went on our own vacation…" Leo added. The plan had been for them to visit some of Grandpa's old stomping grounds from when he was in the war. A history lesson and vacation combined.

"Yes. There wasn't anything I could do. I just hoped that your dad would make a good king."

"So, what happened?" They had never talked about the accident.

"It's only speculation…I mean, it's just a guess."

"Uh huh."

"Well, I think they tried to open the return portal while the train was in motion. They probably tried to force your father into the portal. I told you they were young." She gripped his hands tighter.

"If they tried to use a portal while in motion, the extra variance could knock the portal out of stasis. We figured that instead of returning them to Elonce, it threw off time and place at that point, sending the entire train car into and out of flux. Jean and Gary must have realized, and tried to shut it down. By the time they closed down the portal it was too late – the train had derailed as it was no longer where it was supposed to be."

His giggles were totally gone now.

"It was a pretty bad accident. Over 39 people died when the train derailed."

"Including my parents." Leo added.

It took Grans a little while before she could continue. He wasn't about to rush her.

The wind blowing across the river toward them made the air cool and relatively fresh. For really fresh air or water nowadays, you had to go to a National Park. The cities were too polluted – even in a small town in the Midwest. Leo sat with his eyes closed, missing his parents. It seemed that this dream world was responsible for his whole life.

"So it was your friends that killed my parents?" Leo said. *But if this is just a fantasy, why am I getting angry?*

"Do you think they meant for that to happen? It was an accident" she almost yelled. He couldn't remember ever seeing his grandmother angry. It shocked him.

He realized this was causing her pain.

He always thought of his own loss, but he didn't think about the fact that it was also her son, her only child, and daughter-in-law that died that day. He thought about how they had never discussed the accident, and how he had thought it was because they were afraid it would be too painful for a young boy to take. Now he realized it was too painful for his grandparents.

"No. I'm sorry, but this sucks," he said.

"I know. But it's not all about you. Or even about your parents. Or Grandpa."

They sat in silence for a long time.

"So that leaves team three," she said finally.

"Tell me about them. They'll want me to go back because I look like Gramps did, right?"

"Imrial and John. They were the best of us. That's probably why they picked the best assignment – 'luck follows talent'." He had heard that saying many times in his youth…and he still didn't know exactly what it meant.

"John's pretty plain, not in a bad way, but he doesn't stand out. There's nothing special or odd about him. Well, except maybe his ears. They do stick out from his head a bit." Grans smiled mischievously. It was cute.

She always had a hard time saying negative things about people.

Leo waited for more.

"His eyes are pretty intense and his mouth pouts, so he usually looks like he's upset. Like people here look when they're disappointed with something." Leo was surprised by the intimacy of the description. He had expected the usual – hair color, height, skin tone, any distinguishing marks.

"OK, but how am I supposed to recognize him? Look for a full lipped, big eared, other-wise normal looking guy?" Leo said smiling.

"Sorry. I notice faces..." she said, as if that should explain it. "He's about 6' 2", has dark straight hair, and brown eyes. He usually has a five-o'clock shadow, but in the shape of a goatee."

"Is that how Gramps would describe him?"

"No," she said.

Leo smiled.

"Your grandfather never met John."

"Hmph."

"Leo this is real. I'm not making this up."

"Sorry. Go on," he said.

"Unless he's dressed in the simple clothes we were given, you'll probably not recognize him. Imrial, on the other hand, should be easy to spot. They'll be together."

Leo waited again.

"Immy, that's her nickname, is a cutie." This time her smile was one of conspiracy. "You'd like her."

Leo humored her with a smile of his own.

"She's got great red hair. It's curly, although she normally wears it pulled back in a tight ponytail. She's got very strong features – piercing green eyes, a small, sharp hawk nose, and great cheekbones."

"Is she a model or a military agent?" He smiled at her

again.

"Great, full-bodied lips and…"

"Perfect white teeth?" Leo offered.

"Yes." No sign of anger, or humor. "And before you say it, yes, she has a very strong body – a swimmer's body you'd call it here. She's about 5' 10" and has straight, broad shoulders." Her eyes twinkled as she remembered.

Or imagined.

"So, beauty and the big-ears will be looking for me?"

"Well, yes." Leo could tell she didn't like him calling John 'big-ears.'

"The more I think about it, Jean and Gary didn't just mistake your father for Leonard – the DNA signature was actually your father's." She sat thinking. Something was becoming clear to her - something she hadn't realized before. "The Elder Five identified the three strongest instances of Grandpa's DNA signature. I think they correspond to the three times when Leonard or Leonard's descendants' talents came to maturity. It can happen at various ages depending on the person."

Leo looked as confused as he felt.

"Talents, dear. We all have them, some more than others. Your Grandfather was selected to be the King of Nahasar because he had 7 talents – very rare. Very, very rare."

Leo just shook his head.

"Our talents don't always manifest so others can see them. I only know some of your Grandpa's – like pain threshold. He can take a lot more pain than a normal man and keep on going."

"Does he have super speed?" Leo couldn't help wondering about the dodging bullets part.

"No, no. Talents aren't super powers." She smiled at him, as if he was the one living in a fantasy world.

"That was probably a combination of his talent for avoiding danger and his unerring…you'd call it *sense of direction*. He probably just picked the best route – making it hard for the gunner to hit him."

"So why did he run from being King?"

"I'm not sure. You'll have to ask him. I've always thought it was his avoidance of danger. There was a rumor that someone wanted to assassinate the King of Nahasar. Or maybe he didn't feel ready for the pressures of rulership. It's not an easy thing, being King. I'm really not sure."

They nodded at each other.

"He might not even know why himself," she said finally.

This made a lot of sense to Leo. He always felt like he didn't have a choice – that what he did, or thought, was not due to a conscious decision – it was just the way it was.

"So what are my talents?" Leo asked, forgetting for the moment about Imrial and John or that this was all some sort of shared hallucination his grandparents had developed over decades of marriage.

"What *are* your talents?" And, as was her way, she sat patiently waiting for him to answer.

Leo thought for a while, but couldn't think of anything he was really good at – besides basketball or chess. He was pretty good at those.

"I don't know," he finally decided.

"Why didn't you say 'basketball' or 'chess'?"

Leo looked at her, shocked.

"You can read minds? Is that one of your talents?"

Grans smiled.

"No super powers remember? No, I *can* read faces though. I could tell pretty much what you were thinking, but only because of one of *your* talents."

Then he knew. He wasn't sure how to word it though.

"That's right. Honesty. It's one of your talents, and it's accepted as a talent of the wise."

"Great, I guess being a professional poker player is out."

"Is that a real job?"

"I think so. What are my other talents?" He asked.

"I don't know. That one was evident since you were a duckling. Only the Elder Five can read a person's talents. Well, the Elder Five, sometimes the Oracles, and of course the Curator."

"Who?"

"You'll learn all about them in good time."

"Ok, but there must be a way to know. How can you take advantage of your talents if you don't know what they are?" Leo felt the same way he did when he got a Christmas present at Thanksgiving and couldn't open it until December 25th.

"Well, you can sometimes figure them out based on what you're good at…like basketball and chess." Grans wasn't answering the question as much as she was trying to lead him somewhere, and he realized it.

"So, why I'm good at basketball? Or why I'm good at chess?"

"Exactly."

"So, one of Gramps' talents is…languages. That's why he's good at telling stories. I bet he learned to speak fluent English pretty quickly," Leo deduced.

"And French, German, and Italian. He's fluent in over 10 languages." She smiled at him.

"And *you* have the talent of teaching."

"Very good. How'd you know *that*?" This time he didn't think she was teaching, he thought she was actually curious.

"It's one of my talents! Induction," he said. "Like Sherlock Holmes."

"You mean 'deduction,' or more accurately, 'deductive reasoning.'"

"Right," he agreed.

Grans looked a little disappointed.

"There's more." She got his attention back. "Some talents, like genes or traits, are passed down through generations…"

"So if I find out Gramps, my dad's, and your talents, I may be able to figure out what some of mine are," he finished her sentence for her.

"That can be annoying," she said about him interrupting her.

"I thought *I* was the honest one!" he said, feigning insult.

"Where do you think you got it from?" They both laughed. "I think you also have the talent of avoiding danger like your Grandfather. I'm pretty sure that's why you've never had any serious injuries." Leo knew she was referring to his skateboarding.

"I don't think that's enough proof. Skateboarding isn't *that* dangerous."

"I didn't say avoidance of injury," she corrected him.

"That can be pretty annoying, too," he said, smiling at her. She laughed.

"I guess it can. Sorry. It doesn't mean you don't take risks, just that you pick the safest path when there's a fork in the road."

Leo thought about it for a while. There had been times when he went right instead of left and missed being involved in accidents.

"You mean like the time I was at the park? I knelt down to tie my shoelace and a baseball bat went sailing over my head. It would have hit me for sure." Some kid hitting shag flies to his younger brother had lost control of the bat and it went flying. He hadn't even had time to yell a warning.

"Yes, like that. I've noticed a few times where that type of thing has happened," his grandmother offered.

"That was just a lucky coincidence," he said.

"Really?" she asked.

He thought harder and remembered.

"My shoe lace wasn't untied."

"Luck follows talent."

Leo learned that Grans knew four of Grandpa's seven talents; avoiding danger (like him), sense of direction, pain tolerance, and languages. He'd have to ask Gramps about the other three. He knew he had the talents of avoidance, deductive reasoning, and honesty.

He wasn't sure how honesty was a talent – it seemed more like a handicap. It would be good to be able to lie once in a while.

Grans disagreed strongly; she said it was a royal talent. One that was necessary to be a good ruler.

Leo could tell that honesty was one of *her* talents, he was confident that she had never lied to him. That and teaching – she was the best teacher he'd ever had. He wondered how many talents he had. Perhaps he only had three. Grans was sure he had more - something about traits skipping a generation and how it was now obvious he was meant to be king. And if he were to be king, he assuredly must have more than just three talents.

"So, when is team three supposed to come after me?" he asked, surprisingly calm.

"I don't know. I never bothered to learn what time each team was going to – just the order. I knew I was on the first team, Gary and Jean were team two, and Imrial and John were last." It dawned on him that she had gotten the most dangerous assignment - the one most unlikely to succeed.

"So how do you know they didn't already come? Maybe they got lost?"

"Or died?" she added.

"Yeah."

"Well, I hope not. They're my friends. But I also don't think so. If I'm right about the DNA signature spikes being when talents manifested themselves strongly then we still have some time. When your Grandfather was in the war, his talents were very powerful – they kept him alive on more than one occasion."

Leo thought of his medals again.

"I believe your father's talents were coming to the forefront on their trip. His were more 'soft' talents. Things that were more subtle, and therefore not as obvious." Leo asked for more with his face and since Grans was good at reading faces...

"Well, it's just a guess. His talents never seemed to show up. I think they had to do with travel. I think he had Gramps' sense of direction and languages, but I'm not sure of the others. Perhaps his talent for languages was coming out because of all the different places they were going - I know he was listening to some language tapes."

"You must be right. His talents, whatever they were, must have been coming out," Leo decided.

"Do you think mine are mani...what did you call it?"

"Manifesting. Becoming strong. Think of it like maturing."

"...or puberty?"

Grans blushed.

"Sure."

"Do you think my talents are maturing?"

"Yes."

He sat and thought for what seemed a very long time. Finally, he deduced what Grans already knew.

"They'll be coming for me soon."

"Yes, I believe they will." Grans smiled at him as she stood up. It was time to go. It was already dark and she wanted to get back to Gramps' side, before visiting hours were over.

It is important to be relaxed. Strangers always seem uncomfortable in their surroundings.

It is important not to look around at everything with wonder and awe. Take a look at specific interesting sites, and linger on them. Examine them fully so that you don't give the appearance of being overwhelmed by unfamiliar surroundings. Instead make it appear that you are studying an anomaly in the familiar.

Don't speak. Nod meaningfully, use gestures, but don't speak. Your accent will give you away. If you must speak, mutter forcefully. Muttering softly will give the appearance of fear. Swagger, don't walk. Jog, don't run. Lounge, don't sit.

Observe those around you and learn from their mannerisms. The extra time you take to fit in will be invaluable in making it possible for you to function in a foreign land.

> - Tips from "How Not To Look Like
> A Tourist," 3rd Edition, Published
> by the House of Noss.

5

He was standing on the corner, discreetly watching the pair walking over the bridge. He glanced down at the picture again. It wasn't a great photo. Leonard Hardy obviously didn't like having his picture taken. John figured it wasn't just modesty. The original picture was of a honeymooning couple at the Museum Island. In the near background, a young Leonard Hardy was in line at a food station. It was taken about two years before he ran off. Leonard was cropped out of the photo so that only a three-quarter-view close-up was left. It showed a

disheveled, dirty blond, 5'11 man in need of a shave. He
had a jutting chin with a small cleft in it. He had healthy
looking eyebrows that shaded his eyes, which looked,
well, happy.

Based on the picture, his eyes could be any color, but
based on his family heritage, they were probably brown.

John was sure the young man walking toward the top
of the hill was Leonard, but something wasn't right. He
couldn't stop thinking he recognized the old lady walking
arm in arm with Leonard. She was very familiar. Even
the *way* she walked seemed to strike a chord.

"Is it him?" Imrial said forcefully, as she grabbed his
left elbow. He jumped, dropped the picture, and let out
a gasp. She smiled.

"Wha?"

She smiled even broader.

"Immy, can't you ever be serious?" He picked up the
photo and put it back in his pants pocket. She always
could sneak up on him.

"Of course. It's just that you *never* joke around, so I
have to do more just to balance out our team." To an
observer it would look like they were a playful couple,
with Imrial being a young, irresponsible, joker. However
it wouldn't take too much effort to realize she was a
professional. The whole time she spoke to John, her eyes
were tracing every step their targets took.

"Very funny," John said, as he started off at a quick
trot toward the bridge.

"Not so quickly; give them a little more space." Imrial
suggested.

"But they'll be…"

"Going to the hospital to visit Leonard Hardy," she
said, as she started to walk slowly next to him.

"What are you talking about? That was our target
with…" he started saying, as he turned to look at her.

Imrial kept walking past him.

"With Jenny," she finished his sentence for him.

"What?!" he almost yelled, and then cupped his hand over his mouth. He hurried to catch up. She waited at the crest of the bridge. From there she could see the two enter the visitor's lobby of the hospital.

"What in the world are you talking about?" he said, pulling the picture from his pocket again to make his point. "*That* was Leonard Hardy!"

She just watched until they disappeared into the hospital. Once they were out of sight, she turned to John who was still pointing to the picture.

"Didn't you recognize the old woman?"

"She looked familiar, but…" he thought about it. "Jenny? You said she's Jenny?"

Imrial knew it took a while for John to process things, but once he did he was quite sharp.

"But if that's Genevieve, then who was the boy?"

"It was Jenny alright. You could tell by the way her head bobbed as she walked. Obviously Leonard is an old man now."

He had never realized how strong her talent of observation was. John just kept staring at the picture.

"The boy must be his grandson. Too much of a resemblance to be anything else – unless it's their son."

"But, that's not possible. I know we were honed in on Hardy's DNA Signature when we came through, and he was right there in front of us." They had arrived while the pair were deep in conversation – laughing one moment, almost crying the next. They easily slipped out of sight before they were noticed.

"I know. I guess the boy has the same signature."

"But, how did you know about the hospital? How do you know Hardy is even still alive?"

"I just know." She didn't want to take the time to

explain her talent. Imrial could tell, by the way Leo and Jenny spoke to each other on the bench, what the conversation was about without hearing a word.

"Well let's go get him then." John actually took a step toward the hospital. But only one step, then he stopped to see what his partner would do.

"Leonard Hardy's dying." She said.

"What? How can you possibly know *that*?" She ignored the question, since it didn't really matter. What did matter was what they were going to do now.

"I want to talk with Jenny. We didn't come all this way for nothing." It was funny discussing the distance traveled. They knew they had traversed time and space, a distance only few had ever crossed, and none had returned from. She wasn't talented in deduction, but it didn't take a lot of insight to realize that Jenny's team failed, and if Leonard Hardy was still here, so did team two. But what really made it strange was seeing her friend, Jenny.

Imrial and John had just stepped into the portal moments ago, shortly after the other two teams had left. Less than three hours ago, she had wished Jenny luck and given her a kiss on the cheek. Jenny had whispered in her ear – "see you later." And it had made her want to cry. They knew their chances of survival and return were slim. No one else had ever come back…it was just too chancy. Too many variables. They weren't even sure how the machine really worked! They could easily appear in the middle of a volcano, or in the middle of a busy street to be run over by the vehicles these people used.

"See you later…" She said to herself quietly.

"What?" John had put the picture back in his pocket.

"I said, let's go talk to Jenny."

She started off toward the hospital, with John beside

her. She felt in her pocket for her item – the small metal slug. It was extremely cold to the touch, but it made her feel warmer touching it.

When they exited the elevator on the fourth floor, they turned right and headed to the nurse's station. Like most hospitals, everything was white, clean, and smelled of disinfectant. And like most places with the sick and dying, it made Imrial a bit queasy. It may have been the smell, or her determination to speak to Jenny, that caused her to be less observant than normal.

She took a deep breath before speaking to the nurse at the desk.

"Good day, we're looking for Leonard Hardy?"

The nurse looked up at her with a question in her eyes, but she didn't ask one.

"Room 425. Down the hall, second door on your left." She pointed the way to go.

"Thank you," Imrial said, turning to go. She thought the nurse had looked at her as if she were odd because of her clothes. From what she had seen in the town and the lobby, she thought they fit in all right. Their clothes were a little odd, but it seemed in this place that more than a few people dressed 'differently.' When she turned to go, she realized what it was that had drawn the nurse's curiosity. It must have been her use of 'we,' since she was alone. John was nowhere to be seen. She must have stood looking around the area a little longer than normal because the nurse started to come around the desk.

"Are you alright, sweetie?"

Imrial gave her a little laugh. "Yes, my boyfriend must have gotten lost in the lift."

"Oh. Ok. I'll keep an eye out for him." The nurse hesitated, picked up a stack of clipboards with medical charts on them and headed off down the other corridor. Imrial wondered how she would keep an eye out for John if she wasn't there, but decided that the nurse would know everything that happened on the floor, even if she wasn't at the desk.

"Thanks," Imrial said as she headed the other way down the hall toward room 425. She'd have to figure out where John went off to later. She had to talk to Jenny about the mission. When she reached the room, she pushed the door in slowly and quietly. Leonard Hardy was laying in the bed, hooked up to a couple of machines, tubes running out of his arm. Genevieve was holding his hand, sitting next to him. She was speaking softly to him.

Imrial took a quick assessment of the situation. She knew her assumption had been right. Leonard Hardy, the next King of Nahasar, the man she was sent to retrieve, was dying.

I guess you don't have to worry about an assassination plot…

Odd, she thought – she was still dealing with the whole situation as if it was yesterday when Hardy left. In this here and now, it had been a lifetime since he had escaped from his responsibilities.

Genevieve looked up.

Imrial knew she had been quiet. There was no way Jenny heard her – but they had been friends for a long time. She wasn't surprised Jenny could sense her presence. Jenny held up a finger, meaning *'wait a moment,'* and continued talking to the sleeping man who refused to be King. Imrial let the door close quietly. She looked around the hall. Still no John.

Hmph. Where are you? The hall was empty.

After a few minutes, a much older version of Genevieve De Scioncia than she last saw in Elonce, came out of the room. Her eyes were the same, though. They sparkled with happiness and excitement at seeing her old friend.

"We have to talk," they said simultaneously.

"This way." Jenny led her back down the hall toward the elevators.

Once the doors to the car closed, Genevieve hugged her. "I missed you so much!"

Imrial didn't know quite what to say. For her, it was just over a couple of hours ago that she last saw her friend. But, she returned the hug and showed surprising restraint in not bombarding Jenny with questions.

When they reached the first floor, Jenny finally released her. There were tears in her eyes. Jenny grabbed her hand and they walked to the cafeteria.

"You've become much more emotional," Imrial said carefully.

"Old age does that to you." Genevieve laughed a little. It was definitely a strange situation. "Would you like a drink? Orange soda's your favorite, right?"

"Yes." Imrial followed her through a small corridor of utensils, plates, and trays. They stopped at a machine, which dispensed an orange colored carbonated liquid. Jenny filled two glasses and walked to the cashier. She paid for the drinks and led Imrial to an isolated table in a corner.

She put the glasses down, one in front of each of them.

Imrial tasted it, and then downed half the glass.

Jenny just watched. Both hands holding her glass, as if to cool them.

"Just like home, except no pulp." Imrial said, and then finished the glass. Jenny smiled and waited.

Imrial knew Jenny's ways, but was surprised that she showed *that* much patience. She used to wait for a few seconds, but that was all. She'd normally be asking her tons of questions or telling her everything there was to tell by now.

"You've changed," Imrial said.

Jenny knew she didn't mean her appearance.

"Yes, I've grown." More waiting. Imrial wasn't sure she liked the new Jenny. She was much more like the Elder Five than was healthy.

"So, Leonard Hardy is dying." Imrial said.

"Yes."

"And you have been with him since you came here? I doubt you just recently found him yourself."

"Yes."

"But Stan? Your partner? Dead, I presume?"

"Yes. He had the chip but it wasn't on his body, so I couldn't come home. I believe Gary and Jean are also dead. I'm the only one left."

"Hmmm." It was Imrial's turn to listen.

"It seems we were right to think the last one would be the first back."

"That's the way." Imrial said.

"But Leonard's not going back. He'd die before you got him to the coronation."

"Then what? I mean, we were sent to bring him back. The prophecy! What are we supposed to do? Go back in time and try again?" She immediately regretted blurting it all out. It showed her fears and worse, she hadn't half the patience that Jenny now had.

And still Jenny waited.

It made Imrial a little angry, but she knew Jenny was doing the right thing, letting her work it out for herself. It was just hard to realize that her good friend, her peer from a few hours ago, was now her senior by a good forty-plus years.

"No, they're not going to send anyone else. This is the shot they took," Imrial decided.

Jenny only sipped her drink in response.

"So, if not Leonard, then…"

Jenny looked up at her. Jenny knew her friend had always been quick.

"The boy? But Jenny, how can he be ready?"

Jenny put the glass down and wove the fingers of her hands together. She leaned back in the chair.

"I guess he's as old as Leonard was when he was supposed to be King?" Imrial continued.

"Just a few years younger," Jenny finally said. Thankful for the reprieve, Imrial took the glass from in front of Jenny and gulped down half of the remainder.

"He'll do fine. He's trying to come to grips with the whole thing – he doesn't quite believe it."

"What's not to believe? That his father – or is it grandfather?" Imrial asked.

"Grandfather," Jenny said.

"That his grandfather came from a different world, in a different time? That he ran away from being king of unarguably the most powerful of the five nations of Elonce? That his grandmother was sent back to fix it by bringing Leonard back, and instead she, what? Married him?" Imrial guessed.

Jenny just nodded.

"And now someone would be coming to take him back to be king in his grandfather's place? What's not to believe?"

Jenny laughed softly. There was much more to Leo's life, but that was the crux of the matter.

"He's a good boy, and talented" was all she offered.

"He'd better be, to rule Nahasar," Imrial said.

She saw Jenny tense and then relax, a shimmer of pride and happiness spread across her face.

"So, are you going to introduce me?" Imrial said, turning around to look at Leo.

"I guess I'll have to."

It's funny how you can believe almost anything when you're tired, isolated, and the person telling you the unbelievable fully believes it herself.

Amazing really. Leo would swear that he was ready to jump on a spaceship and travel to Elonce with his grandmother when she was telling him the story. But, as soon as they had crested the top of the bridge, his sanity returned. It was a nice fantasy that he allowed himself to get swept up in. He figured he knew how cults worked now. The fanatical leader isolates his (it always seems to be men leading them) subjects from the rest of the world, and then they spin their impossible dream with so much sincere belief that the followers just get wrapped up in it.

Scary.

Once they entered the lobby of the hospital, he was back to normal. There was no way he could still be caught up in his grandmother's fantasy when the real world was all around him. The noise, bustle, and other sane people in the lobby finished breaking the spell.

He had to smile at himself.

He didn't let Grans see him. It might hurt her feelings if she thought he was laughing at her. She really believed it all. He wondered if his grandfather told her the story so many times that she finally started believing it.

Leo took Grans up to see Leonard Hardy, the reluctant King of fairyland. He loved his grandfather, but he couldn't help making light of his fantasy world. He didn't want to think of him as dying – crazy was better than dying.

Anything was better.

Leo left Grans and headed down to the lounge on the second floor. He figured she could use some time alone with her husband. Funny, he never thought of them as husband and wife – just his grandparents.

The lounge had a big screen television, with cable.

The grand-folks didn't believe in cable or satellite. In fact, they barely believed in TV at all.

He was lucky; there wasn't anyone in the lounge – so he had total control of the remote.

After an hour and a half, a cute girl came in with her mom. Leo sat up. She didn't even look at him. That's one of the worst parts of being in the hospital. Most people you meet there are sick, dying, or sad because of someone sick or dying. Either way, *there's no chance for romance.*

Leo smiled at his poetic powers and slouched back on the couch.

Fifteen minutes later, another family of visitors came in. A dad and three rug rats. They were loud, annoying, and all over the place. So, he did the only honorable thing – he turned on the Cartoon Network and gave the remote to the dad.

Time to check on Grans.

When Leo got to the fourth floor, the nurse at the station told him that his grandmother had gone down the elevator with a young woman a few minutes ago.

When he reached the first floor, he looked for her in the lobby. He thought she might be waiting for him to walk her home. No luck. He headed toward the cafeteria. It seemed they had been spending a lot of time there lately.

When he spotted Grans, she was waving him over. He got about half way across the room when a sharp pain hit his stomach. It didn't make him double over or anything; it just felt like someone stuck him with a needle in his belly button. He pulled his shirt away from his skin thinking there must have been a pin or something in the shirt. Leo was feeling around the shirt for the cause of the pain and didn't notice that Grans and her friend were both standing up, coming toward him.

"What is it Leo?" Grans asked, with more worry in her voice than he thought appropriate.

"What's what?" He asked, giving her a smile to let her know he was all right.

"Something's the matter. I can see it on your face." Grans said. Her friend stood on her left, just a step behind her. Her face said she saw the same thing, whatever it was.

"Something's just sticking me. It's probably a pin or something in my shirt." He said, feeling a little defensive. "It's no big deal."

Great. Nice first impression.

They both looked at him as if he had a gushing head wound.

"What?" He asked, getting annoyed.

He tried not to look at the girl...she was just a girl...around his age. But he kept glancing at her.

"*Is* there a pin or something in your shirt?" she asked.

He hadn't been able to find one, if it was. The pain pricked at his stomach again.

"Ow," he said. He didn't want to. He wanted to act like he hadn't felt anything, but it just came out.

Great second impression.

"It's not a pin." Grans said decisively.

Her friend seemed to be scanning the room. Leo couldn't get eye contact. He was striking out before he even got to the plate with every girl he saw!

"It's not about any of us. The room's clear," she said.

Leo thought her voice matched her looks - very nice.

A little bossy, like she was used to being in charge, but it was nice. She also had very pretty red hair pulled back from her face.

"Clear?" Leo asked. There were at least 10 other people in the room. He didn't know what she meant, and he didn't care. He was just hoping she'd look at him if he said something. She finally stopped looking around and settled her eyes on Grans. Oh well. He could still see they were pretty eyes.

"No," Grans agreed, "it must be Leonard." She started off at full speed. Her friend was already in step with her before Leo could say a word. He let go of his shirt and followed, trying to figure out what was going on.

When they got to the elevator, Leo watched the girl with the nice voice, red hair, and pretty eyes run toward the stairs and slam the door inward with a bang. He came up beside Grans.

"What's going on? Did you say something was wrong with Gramps?" he asked. The elevator doors opened and they stepped inside.

"Think Leo. Use that newly realized talent of yours – the one where you figure out problems."

Oh no, he thought to himself. He didn't want to think about talents, other worlds, or time portals. He just wanted to know what was going on.

"You mean deductive reasoning, but…" he started.

"Yes, like that Sherlock Holmes character in the movies," she said as they approached the fourth floor. He could read the worry and fear on her face without the use of any talent.

"Grans…" he tried again.

"Think!" She almost growled it. Leo had never seen her lose her patience before. Between that and the look on her face, he knew something was really wrong.

Instead of thinking he started pressing the button for the fourth floor over and over and over.

The doors opened and she moved at her top speed toward Gramps' room.

Part of his mind was surprised not to hear a nurse complain about visiting hours being over, another part made sure he followed Grans without walking into a wall or wheelchair, and the rest of his mind finally did as requested – it was in thinking mode.

Leo found it wasn't a deductive reasoning question as much as it was a need to use his memory. Grans and the girl were worried when they saw his face…no, when they saw that he felt a pricking pain. Grans knew it wasn't a pin even before he didn't find one. It was also before the pain hit again, when he was still holding his shirt away from his body. Therefore they both knew it meant something; it was a sign they both understood. And then he remembered. He had felt that pain a few times before. One time was when it made him look down and see that his shoelace was untied.

Only it wasn't.

And if the danger wasn't dealing directly with him, it must be with someone close to him.

Leo ran the rest of the way and beat Grans to the door.

The pretty girl he had seen with Grans was covering Gramps' eyes. She did it gently. She walked by him without a word and left the room.

If he had looked at her, he might have noticed that she looked as if she wanted to kill someone.

Grans walked in and patted Leo's arm before she went over to her husband. She was calm. Calmer than Leo. He wanted to scream, cry, yell, and throw something. He couldn't believe Gramps had actually died. He took a deep breath, spun around and went out of the room. Someone was going to pay for this, what kind of hospital was this? Gramps was hooked with wires and tubes – one of those things should have alerted the nurses to his condition. Where were they? Someone was going to pay for this!

The girl wasn't outside the room.

Leo didn't care where she was. He wanted to yell at someone.

"Hello!" He yelled as he headed to the nurses' station.

"Hello! Anyone here? My grandfather died, and no one cares?" The more he yelled, the more he wanted to yell some more.

"Someone's going to lose their job!" He shouted. He wasn't sure what he was yelling. He wouldn't have been surprised if he started yelling about green eggs and ham. He just wanted to yell. He just wanted to break something.

"Someone's going to pay!" He yelled as he reached the station and slammed his fist down on the counter.

"Someone already has." Imrial spoke in a near whisper. It wasn't a whisper, though. She was just speaking calmly, slowly, deliberately. Probably to get him to stop yelling.

It worked.

That and the sight of the dead nurse on the floor behind the desk. The girl was covering the dead nurse's eyes the same way she had done to Gramps.

"You need to go back and help Jenn…your grandmother." She stood up and walked toward him. Slowly. He couldn't take his eyes off the nurse. Gramps was in a hospital bed. He had died a little earlier than expected, but he had *been* dying. This nurse hadn't been dying. She was a relatively young, healthy woman. She probably had children at home, a husband that would miss her, and friends. He thought of his parents and a mix of sadness and anger filled him.

"What happened?" He asked, still staring at the nurse. He noticed a pool of blood under her head.

"She had an accident. Now go help your grandmother. I'll call for help," she said as she lifted the receiver of the phone and slid sideways a little so he couldn't see the nurse. Leo looked at her.

She was beautiful. He wasn't sure if it was the excitement or how cool she seemed under fire, but she was beautiful. He couldn't stop staring at her.

"Go," she said one more time.

And he did.

Assassinations can be said to have originated as far back as when Cain killed his brother Abel. The world has not known peace since. While murder has been accepted to be a grievous crime, assassinations have stood out as the most heinous of murders with cause (see note h. for wars, mass murders, and terrorism). From Julius Caesar to John F. Kennedy, assassinations have plagued the world. The war to end all wars, started after the assassination of Archduke Franz Ferdinand. Assassinations generally change the world - and most would say, not for the better.

- "Assassinations and Their Fallout,"
a study by David Willoughby for
Master of Arts thesis, University of
Notre Dame

6

Leonard Hardy was an easy target, trapped in a hospital bed.

This didn't bother John, easy was good.

The nurse was an unexpected problem, but he was trained to deal with the unexpected. His ability to deal with rapid change was one of the reasons he was selected for a retrieval team.

His lack of feelings and willingness to kill were the reasons he was hired to ensure Leonard Hardy never took the throne of Nahasar.

But now what?

If he could get the memory chip away from Imrial, he was home free.

At least that's what he thought, until he saw the kid again. John wasn't the sharpest tool in the shed, but when he saw the kid leaving the hospital with Genevieve and Imrial, he knew. The kid was a dead ringer for the photo.

Yeah, the kid wasn't Leonard Hardy, but he would be King if he went back.

He was right the first time. That meant he had killed two people for nothing. That didn't bother him either. What did bother him was that by now, Imrial would have figured out that he wasn't what she thought. They'd all be on their guard.

He liked Imrial. The rest of the stupid agents he could do without, but Imrial had treated him like a partner. Well, really, why shouldn't she? He was her partner. They had drawn lots and they were paired up with the best of the slots. She didn't know he was a border-line psychotic, waiting to reach full bloom. She didn't know that he had repressed desires to kill for the fun of it. All she knew was that there was another agent unlucky enough to get the assignment of a lifetime. One that likely wouldn't end well.

He knew no one had traveled in time and come back to tell any tales. He knew none of their chances looked good…but that was one of his strengths. One of the benefits of being a bit more than a little off center. He really didn't care if any of them – including himself, made it back. Nope. It would be a grand adventure no matter what.

The opportunity to kill the future King, to change history, was just an extra incentive. And now that he had killed two people, he was giddy with excitement. This was fun.

He tried to focus on the job. His real job. Watching them walk out of the hospital, he knew that job just became harder. Hard wasn't so bad, but easy would have been better.

He made a mental note of his new task list.

One - get the chip from Imrial.

It didn't bother him that he hadn't thought of doing that before. He knew he should have asked to carry it from the beginning. But he understood that no one was perfect. He was ok with his own mistakes. He forgave himself readily. As long as he learned from those mistakes he was ok with it. He'd learn from this and not let anyone else hold the key to his future again.

Two - kill the kid.

It was the best way to ensure he succeeded, and, well, it would be fun. Leonard was old and dying. The nurse was too quick. He wanted the killing to last this time. Someone young like the kid would make a much more spectacular death.

Three - go home and get his payment.

The order of the first two could be interchanged, but going home was definitely last. Wealth wasn't the main reason he took the job, but he had plans for the payment already. Of course having some dirt on a future king, like the fact that he had the rightful heir murdered, would be even more valuable.

He wasn't sure what he'd do with all that money. He didn't know if there were opportunities back home for an assassin. What he did know was that he'd have to find a way to do more of it. He watched them go down the hill.

He waited until they were a good two blocks ahead before he started following them.

To have the capacity to kill without hesitation requires the pre-belief that the killer can take life without guilt or regret. This notion, that taking a life can be done without regret, while possible, has never been confirmed as having existed except in instances where the subject exhibited clearly sociopathic behavior.

- Dr. Johansson Philips, Doctor of Criminal Psychology, Capella University

7

When they reached the house, Jenny put on a pot of coffee. Imrial and Leo sat at the kitchen table, silent. No one wanted to start the conversation which they all knew was inevitable.

Jenny gave Imrial and Leo each a cup of coffee and sat down, without one for herself.

Leo slid his cup toward Grans.

"No, I can't hold anything down right now," she said. She put a warm hand on his wrist. He left the cup halfway between them, not knowing what to do with it.

She knows I don't drink coffee. She must be really out of it.

They all sat in silence for a while. In different ways, the death of Leonard Hardy affected each of them.

"Leo, your grandfather didn't die of natural causes. He was murdered," Imrial started the discussion.

Leo looked at the woman with the red hair, sipping a cup of coffee. She was telling him his grandfather was killed as calmly as if she were telling him what time it was.

"And who exactly are you?" He couldn't help it, he felt like having a fight with someone, and it didn't matter if she was pretty or not. She'd do.

Grans just sat, staring at her hands.

"My name is Imrial. I'm here to help."

Leo just sat there. His mouth wasn't hanging open. His eyes weren't "wide with surprise." Part of him knew who this woman was. Part of him, deep down, had believed Gramps and Grans.

Part of him had not wanted to believe.

But why not? Who wouldn't want to find out their family was special? That his grandparents were actually from a different world, a different time? That he was actually the grandson of the heir to a throne?

Leo wasn't excited.

He wasn't scared.

He was struck dumb. He couldn't hear or speak. He just sat staring at the red haired woman across from him. After a while, her lips moved.

No sound though. His mind was moving too fast. No, that wasn't the problem. His thoughts were all over the place, he couldn't focus.

She was definitely the most beautiful girl he'd ever seen.

Imrial? The Imrial from Grans' story? This was too much to swallow.

They waited. Finally, after what seemed forever, Leo's mind cleared.

Then it hit him...the logical answer. Of course her name was Imrial – every good story is based on some amount of truth. She must have been a nurse or maybe even a police officer. Yeah, that made sense with Grans' story. He didn't know how she had met Grans, but obviously they weren't childhood friends - their age difference was the same as his and Grans'. He wondered if Imrial knew about the stories Grans told about her.

"Sorry, what did you say?" he finally attempted.

Leo wondered where she was from. Her accent seemed foreign, but he couldn't place it.

"I was saying that I was sorry about your

grandfather."

"Thanks." Leo turned toward Grans, but she wasn't sitting next to him any longer. She had stepped out of the room while he was in his fog. Leo looked around the room and started to get up.

"She's in the...the bath," Imrial finally said.

"She's taking a bath?" he asked.

"No, she's..." she seemed to be having trouble.

"Using the bathroom?" he helped.

"Yes, I guess that's right," she smiled. Leo sat back down.

"So, how do you know Grans?"

"Jenny? I've known her for years. We're good friends. Maybe best friends." Leo had never heard anyone call her Jenny before. Grandpa always called her 'Jen' or something sappy like 'my love.'

"So, how do you know Grans?" he asked again. She hadn't answered the question. He guessed he was still angry about Gramps dying. Dying? She said he had been murdered! Leo didn't wait for the answer.

"What do you mean Gramps was murdered?"

She seemed relieved to change the subject, even if it was about murder.

"He was smothered. There were signs."

"Are you a cop?" he asked, a bit of anger and disbelief in his voice. Leo half expected her to say she was an international police woman - like Interpol, or even a foreign spy.

"Maybe," she said. He thought she meant to say 'sort of' but she didn't know the right words. "I know about murder. Whoever killed your grandfather also killed the nurse."

He remembered the nurse lying behind the desk.

"Why would anyone kill a dying old man?" Leo asked with disgust.

"What has Jenny told you about Leonard Hardy's past? About her past?" she asked. Leo didn't like where this was going.

"What does that have to do with anything?"

"Did they tell you anything that was hard to believe?" she asked.

"What? The stories about Elonce? About her being a military agent sent back to…" There was no shock or confusion on her face. She knew the stories, too.

"Yes. What did she tell you about me?"

"Nothing real. You're supposed to be an agent, too, sent here to take Gramps back, but you'd probably want to take me instead," Leo told her. Again, no surprise on her face.

"Especially now that he's dead," she said calmly.

"Yes, I guess so. What's wrong with Grans? Why does she believe all that?"

"I'm worried for her. And you." Imrial said, once again, avoiding a question. Then he realized she had avoided almost all of his questions.

"Thanks," Grans said from behind him. She walked back into the room. "I don't think I'm a target. But Leo…well, we have to move fast."

She walked over to the coffeepot and poured herself a fresh cup. The other one was where Leo had left it, now cold.

Leo looked at Imrial, wondering how much she'd humor Grans. If there really was some lunatic trying to kill them, they wouldn't want to waste time trying to get Grans back to reality. It dawned on him - this was too much like a bad horror movie. Where were the police?

"Why don't we just call the police? What happened when you called them at the hospital?" he asked Imrial. "Why haven't they shown up to question us?"

She ignored his questions.

"Jenny, we'll have to leave right away. Do you have transportation?"

"Did you even call them?" Leo asked.

Imrial walked over to Grans and said something softly to her. Something Leo couldn't hear.

Grans turned to him and soothingly said, "Leo, can you drive us?"

"What? Where?" Everything was moving a little too fast. "What did she say? What did she do?"

"Dear, we have to go," Grans said softly, but her body had tensed up. She looked ready to slap him.

"What did she do?" Leo yelled.

Then she did slap him. Funny, he knew it was coming, but he couldn't bring himself to dodge it.

Imrial finally answered a question, "I did what I had to. Now, you have to do what you have to do,"

So he did.

It probably wasn't what she meant. But, he did what was necessary and began to cry.

He cried, hard. His grandfather, who for the last eight years had been his father, had died - been murdered. He was gone. Grans held him while he sobbed like a little kid. He buried his wet face in her shoulder and cried. He was so tired. He was tired of losing his loved ones. He was tired of the confusion. And he was mad at the world – but especially mad at the person who killed his grandfather.

After a while, Grans said, "Are you ready?"

"Give me a minute." It was his turn to use the bathroom. He needed to wash up.

He needed a fresh start.

Somehow, he knew, he would never have the luxury of crying over the dead again.

Leo washed his face and took some time to gather himself.

Grans gave Imrial a jacket to wear -- the nights could get pretty cool. Leo thought guys didn't notice clothes (unless they're missing) on a woman. It didn't hit him until he saw her putting on the jacket that her outfit matched Grans' description of the agents' traveling clothes perfectly. Her top was a simple, green, pullover tunic-looking thing. Her green pants looked like sweats, but they weren't made out of the same material as sweats were. They were smooth, like slacks. And her shoes. They looked like something out of a karate movie.

He still wasn't sure what was going on. He wasn't sure if Imrial was a cop, a friend of Grans, or a lunatic from the Elonce cult. He wasn't sure if they were in any real danger, or if the police had ever been called. There was a lot he wasn't sure about.

It was easier to think about what he *was* sure of.

He was sure his grandfather was dead. He was sure there was a nurse lying on the floor behind her desk with blood pooling under her. He was sure he was going to drive Grans and Imrial wherever they wanted to go. Well, at least *they* thought so. He figured he'd drive them to the county sheriff's office.

He pulled Grandpa's old Ford out of the driveway and headed South out of town.

"Where are we going?" He asked. The state police had a station about eight miles outside of town. Their jurisdiction covered three neighboring towns so they put the station equally distant from all three. All of the county offices were there, the fire department, sheriff's station, and a small airport. They were all housed on what used to be excellent farm land.

"The airport." Grans said.

His luck was getting better.

He wondered if they were running from someone or running to something. Either way, the destination would work. Leo would have no trouble getting them to the police station. Once there, he would deal with getting them out of the car and inside the station.

One thing at a time...

As they entered what passed as a highway in their small town, he stepped on the gas and pushed the car to 50 miles per hour.

Grans was in the back of the car and Imrial was next to him riding shotgun. He didn't look directly at her - partly because he still didn't know anything about her, partly because he didn't quite trust her, and partly because she was beautiful. That and he didn't want to get into an accident – that would be too much to handle. He kept his eyes on the road, with some serious effort.

But even with his eyes looking forward, he couldn't help notice that she had taken something out of a pocket and was flipping it. Like an old style video game token.

"What are we running from?" Leo finally decided to ask.

"John," Imrial said simply. She turned and looked out the back window.

He couldn't quite accept this.

"John? As in your partner?"

"Yes, my teammate," she said, still watching behind them.

"And you're from..."

She wouldn't finish it for him. She sat looking out the back window, waiting.

"Elonce," he whispered. He didn't think she had heard him.

"Yes."

Leo laughed.

Either the both of them were crazy, and Grandpa had

been too, or it was all true.

"So, why are we running? Why didn't we just use that coin thingy back at the house?"

"It's not that simple. John was nearby, and the reception was weak. If we tried there, he'd have time to kill you before the transfer was complete."

He stifled another laugh. This was unbelievable.

"Reception?"

"Yes. There are places, in time and space, where a portal can be formed cleaner than others. If we are in a place and time that has a strong reception, we can slip through in seconds, otherwise it can take up to fifteen minutes."

She wasn't playing with the coin. She was *reading* it somehow.

She hadn't looked at him once, she was still studying the traffic behind them.

"Can this go faster?" She asked.

"Faster? Is he following us?" he asked.

"He's coming up pretty fast. I don't think he's planning on just following us."

Grans took a peek back, too. "I take it one of his talents is with machinery," she guessed.

"He can drive pretty much any vehicle made," Imrial answered, with a twinge of admiration in her voice.

"Great!" Leo said. He had no admiration for him. He only had hatred. John killed his grandfather, and now he wanted to kill all of them. Leo stepped on the gas. The traffic was light in front of them, so he had no trouble accelerating.

"We'll need to teleport, now!" Imrial said.

"No, not while we're moving," Leo said.

"Too dangerous. We'll need to pull over," Grans said, agreeing with him.

"We may not have time," Imrial said, and turned to

look out the front window. "We need to go a lot faster." She was scanning the traffic, trying to come up with a plan.

Leo pushed up to seventy-five, but he was hesitant. He didn't like speeding.

"Faster!" Imrial almost yelled in his ear. She shoved the coin into her pocket.

He wasn't fast enough. John slammed his car into their rear, jarring them all back, then forward. Leo lost control of the wheel, just for a moment. They swerved into the oncoming traffic lane before he could pull them back. A truck swung right, away from them, and he barely got the car back into their lane. He slammed on the gas.

They had a little space between them. Hitting them made John lose a lot of momentum.

The car whined with the effort, he was going to flood the engine.

"Easy," Imrial said.

Leo let off the gas for a second, and then reengaged the pedal, gradually building up more speed.

"Hold on!" Imrial commanded.

John's car hit them again, this time in the left rear. It sent them spinning to the right. The car careened over a short curb, over a grassy section and into a nearly empty shopping market parking lot. Leo turned the wheel into the spin, stepped on the gas, and was able to pull out of it.

All instinct.

Before he had time to be proud of himself, he saw John coming at them from the side. He was going to ram them solid on the driver's side.

Leo calmly stepped on the gas, in control this time. They pulled away, almost in time. John hit them in the side, by the rear. They spun again, and Leo pulled them out of it again. This time they ended up with John in front of them.

"Stop!" Imrial yelled.

Leo guessed she wanted to use the chip and get away while they had a chance…he had other ideas.

He pushed the pedal again.

"Stop! We can escape!" she yelled.

Leo grabbed the wheel tightly, and leaned forward.

"Hold on!" He yelled back at her.

John had stopped. He was backing up, turning to continue his attack.

Leo took him by surprise.

Okay, so I lost it, Leo thought to himself.

He forgot about Grans, or Imrial, or himself. He wasn't scared. He was angry and he wanted to fight back.

Leo caught John's car flush on the driver's side. John's car skipped sideways into a parked minivan. It stopped, threatening to flip on its side until the minivan stopped it. It was like in a movie - the side windows of the van exploded out and covered everything in little pieces of safety glass.

The impact threw the three of them around in the car and then rolled back about twenty feet. The front of the car was crushed. They looked like a demolition derby entry, the back and front of the car were crumpled.

And then like everything else in his life, the car died.

Leo turned the ignition and the old Ford gave a few coughs. He tried again. No luck.

Okay.

John wasn't moving, and Leo wanted to make that condition permanent.

No problem.

He unbuckled and opened his door.

Okay.

"Wait. Leo, wait," Imrial said, holding her forehead. Blood was flowing slowly from underneath her hand.

"Why?" he asked, staring at John's car. Leo had seen too many movies where the killer got away when you were sure he was down for the count.

You've got this.

"Because Jenny needs help." He didn't hear anything from the back seat. No movement, no moans or groans. Just silence and that scared him more than if she were screaming in pain.

"Later," he said. Leo didn't want to see how badly she was hurt – it might stop him from what he had to do.

"Now," Imrial said. "She needs help now."

He stayed like that, one foot out of the car, on the pavement, hand on the open door handle. His other hand on the steering wheel for leverage. It seemed like forever. He kept staring at John's unmoving silhouette.

"Where? The hospital?" he asked.

"No. They'll have a medical team waiting for us when we return."

"At the hospital?"

"No. Elonce."

"You go." He started out of the car again.

She touched the hand on the steering wheel, softly.

"I can't. I need your help." He chanced a glance at her. "You need to pick her up. I'm hurt."

She was keeping her other hand against her body. It hung limply. The wound on her forehead wasn't that bad, but he figured the wrist was broken.

"Please," she said.

"But he'll get away" he said, his voice rising slightly.

"No, he'll be trapped here."

"He'll get away with killing Gramps. And the nurse."

She looked at him. Her eyes looked a little sad, a little scared.

"Please" she said again.

He climbed out of the car, opened the back door, and carefully pulled Grans out and into his arms. She was unconscious. Imrial came around the car and stood beside him. They both took a look toward John's car.

He was still there, leaning forward with his head against the deflated airbag.

"Time to go," she said. She pulled the metal disk out of her pocket. It was totally smooth, no markings of any kind.

Leo could hear sirens winding their way toward them. They had a small audience now, passers-by who had stopped to see if anyone needed help. Two employees from the supermarket stopped gathering carts and were cautiously walking toward them.

"Let's go," Leo said. Either this would work and they actually would be heading off to a different world, or it would make for an interesting visit to the police station.

He had expected more. He thought Imrial would have to do some special incantations, sprinkle pixie dust, or do a ritual dance. All she did was place the coin on the ground and almost whisper some words to it. As she stood back up, the coin jumped twice and began to spin on its side.

"Neat trick," he said to himself. Grans was still out cold in his arms.

Imrial came over to him, gently grabbed his elbow and walked them toward the spinning coin.

He still expected more, but all he could see was a slight wavering in the air above the coin. There seemed to be a large circular area that shimmered. Like when you look at really hot pavement ahead on the road and you think that's what a mirage looks like. That or it was a little blurry. Like he was looking through a big lens. No machinery like Gramps had described.

Imrial ushered Grans and him through first. She never let go of his elbow, so he knew she stepped through right behind them. It was a strange feeling - like walking under water. Everything was a bright blue, and they moved in slow motion. As soon as they were fully "submerged," they stepped out into a different time and place.

Destiny theory has been around for centuries. Its proponents say that it explains everything, while giving credence to the impossible. Its opponents say it leads to apathy and surrender. Destiny theorists propose that everything is predetermined and every thought, action, and reaction has already been decided. You have no real control over your life, all decisions are predetermined and set. Time is not alterable. There is only one path that can be taken and it has already all happened. We just exist in one moment within the fabric of reality. The cloth has already been woven, cut and sewn. The opponents of the theory say that nothing is determined. We have total control over our actions and reactions. We have full responsibility and autonomy in our choices. We are the rulers of our own personal universes and our decisions can and will affect the lives of many others. We can make a difference because anything is possible.

As with most extreme theories, the truth probably lies somewhere between.

- "Musings of a Princess," by
  Princess A. M. Tinneb

8

The Elder Five had a chance to get a soda before the portal began humming with the first of the teams to return. They knew it was a long shot that any of them would succeed, but they had hopes based on the oracle's prediction. Strong hopes indeed.

When the portal opened it meant the machine was activated from some other place and time.

It spun and grew and became the same machine they had seen Leonard Hardy escape through, and the machine they had sent three teams through to bring him back.

As the entry space formed, the First Elder noticed a difference.

"It's orange this time."

The other four nodded. This was all new to them. No one had ever returned from using the machine, and no one had left in their lifetimes.

The large entry point shimmered and then solidified. The whine that the machine made while it took shape was replaced by an incredibly loud whistling sound. It filled the entire hall, shaking glass displays and physically shoving the guards back a few steps from their posts by the ropes. It was a good thing the guards didn't have their weapons drawn as they involuntarily covered their ears with their hands.

"This can't be good," the Third yelled over the din.

Then, the sound of metal click-clacking across metal.

They all took a step back.

The medical team kept backing away. It wouldn't do for *them* to get hurt.

Besides the guards, the two-person medical team, and the Elder Five, there was only one other witness to the day's events at the Museum of Transportation. Santore Noss, the chief advisor to the late King of Nahasar was present to welcome his new ruler. Against the Elder Five's objections, Santore insisted that an official representative of Nahasar be present to ensure no other problems occurred. The story of the escape of Leonard Hardy had quickly spread across Elonce, including the inability of the Elder Five to stop him.

Santore Noss didn't move. He didn't cover his ears. He stood stock still, straight and tall, like a statue. He wore ceremonial white robes with the belt of the house of Nahasar around his waist. He held a royal staff in his right hand, not leaning on it, just holding it firmly about two feet in front of him. His left hand was tucked into his robe, holding the letter of appointment. He was determined to make the right first impression.

For one moment, a hand appeared through the portal, but it was quickly pulled back into the void.

Then there was a scream. It was the worst sound of all. It wasn't a scream like a roller-coaster ride scream, it was a scream of defeat. It was a scream of remorse.

Then, more metal sounds, this time scraping sounds.

Then, more screams. Many more screams. Tears filled the First Elder's eyes.

And then silence.

The portal went dark. It collapsed on itself and closed down. On the dais, two metal disks spun in unison. They came to a stop together. The Fourth Elder rushed over and picked up the return memory chip. He brought it over to the other Elders, who were watching, a bit worried.

"What happened?" the Second yelled, not really expecting an answer. Although the noise had winked out with the machine, his ears were still ringing.

"A failed attempt to return," the Third answered, yelling back. They all nodded.

"What do we do now?" the First shouted.

"More of the same," the Fourth yelled back.

"Yes. We wait," the Fifth agreed, in a normal voice.

They didn't have to wait long.

Ten minutes later, just when the ringing in their heads had finally stopped, the machine began to hum again. The guards immediately clapped their hands over their ears, but there were no loud noises this time. Santore Noss closed his eyes slowly. He said a silent prayer, opened his eyes and stared at the display. He hadn't moved, and he wouldn't move. Not until his new king arrived. The machine spun up as it had before, the portal giving off a soft blue light this time.

Everyone expected loud noises, bright lights, maybe even a scream, but without ceremony or hesitation, Leo Hardy stepped through the portal carrying an old woman. He looked like he had been in a fight. His white t-shirt had bloodstains on the chest and shoulder, and his jeans had a tear below the left knee and another long tear along the right thigh. He had a welt growing on his forehead and his hair was matted with sweat.

Immediately after him came Imrial of Nahasar, looking equally disheveled.

By the time they had stepped off the platform and started toward the ropes, the portal shut down and once again two disks were spinning in unison.

When the guards saw Leo, they broke into applause and cheers. It wasn't professional, but they couldn't help it. This was an amazing event. No one had ever come back from time-traveling before. They moved the ropes back, letting them out of the display area.

Santore Noss executed a perfect, practiced, deep bow.

Imrial took one long stride and moved next to Leo, still holding his elbow, and guided him to a bench across the room. She wasn't happy about having to make him walk the thirty feet to the bench, but it was the closest place he could put Jenny down comfortably.

As Leo was gently setting Jenny on the bench, the Elder Five approached. The Fifth immediately began an examination of Genevieve.

The Third motioned for the medical team to come over and help. The medics seemed a bit nervous. They acted like they had never seen anyone arrive through a time portal before, which of course they hadn't.

The Fourth asked Imrial, "Who is she?"

Before she could answer, everything went crazy.

Santore Noss had managed to get halfway to the

bench from his post when the machine activated again.

Everyone except Leo and the Fifth Elder turned to see what was happening.

The medical team of two stopped approaching and one of them actually took a step back. The guards instinctively covered their ears again.

The machine revved up to full speed and the now familiar blue glow washed across the museum floor. A man stepped through the portal carrying a pistol in his outstretched hand. He anchored his extended arm with his left hand, firmly wrapped around the wrist. He wore a baseball cap over his grey-white, unkempt hair. He wore a camouflage jacket over a hooded sweatshirt, a pair of dirty jeans, and high top tennis shoes. Only his grey-white hair and slow gait gave away his advanced years. That and his raspy, croaking voice.

"Hardy!" It was meant to be a forceful shout, but it came out tired. He coughed twice, spit out some phlegm and tried something else.

"Here's Johnny" he said in a clearer voice. He smiled his best maniacal grin.

The guards were slow to react. Partly because this was another amazing, and unexpected event in an already exciting day, and partly because they had no idea of what the man was holding in his hand. The man's exotic outfit also distracted them.

Imrial, on the other hand, recognized the artifact from her training for the mission. In the Museum of History they had been shown weapons that may resemble what they could encounter on Earth. The thing in the man's hand was a dead-on match for what the display called a "Gun of the Hand."

Imrial also recognized the man.

As John approached Leo, a guard stepped forward. Unfortunately, he approached from John's right side.

"Sir, may I help y…?"

John, let go of his wrist and with a motion quicker than an old man should be capable of, whipped the pistol down into the guard's nose. The sound of his nose breaking was loud enough to be heard over the portal closing.

Two guards started forward to come to their fallen comrade's aid.

John yelled down at the guard, "You talkin' to me?" and grinned. He turned and pointed the gun toward a display made primarily of glass, to his left, and shot once. The loudness of the shot made everyone first focus on John. And then on the display which shattered with a loud crash. The demonstration had the effect he wanted - a stunned hush. Everyone realized that the thing in John's hand was dangerous and destructive.

"Don't move," John said, then swung the muzzle of the gun back to his right and pointed it at the approaching guards. The one in the lead froze, with his sword halfway unsheathed. The others stopped behind him. John motioned with the pistol for them to step away and they moved in the direction he indicated - further to his right.

"Just like a Nahasarian…bringing a knife to a gunfight." He chuckled.

John resumed his march on the group by the bench.

Santore Noss, to his credit, reacted quickly. Or at least that's how he later described it.

When interviewed by Nahasar's media outlet, he explained the part he played. "When I saw the guard go down, I leapt into action. I couldn't afford to hesitate. I had to protect the future king. I tackled him and covered him until it was safe."

What really happened was a little different. Santore did end up knocking Leo down and once on the ground, he was smart enough to realize he was less of a target this way. There was no way he was going to let Leo throw him off, he'd be in the open.

The First through Fourth Elders also reacted quickly to protect the future King of Nahasar. They calmly stepped around the wrestling Santore and Leo, to stand in front of them, shoulder to shoulder.

The Fifth continued to minister to Genevieve.

"Help me, Obi-Wan Kenobi. You're my only hope" John said and smiled again.

Everything was going as he had expected and everyone (except Santore Noss) was reacting as he had predicted.

When the guard approached to inquire if John needed assistance, John wasn't at all surprised. He was a good tactician, and as such, he had already anticipated what was unfolding before him.

But John had forgotten Imrial. She was on the move.

As soon as John had turned to hit the first guard, she was in motion. She grabbed the ceremonial staff out of Santore Noss' hand. He wouldn't let go, so she shoved him. He went sprawling into Leo's legs, knocking them both over.

She bent low and ran to John's left. He was busy telling the guard not to move. As if that were likely after he had broken his nose. She was easily out of his view.

Then he turned in her direction. She slid behind a display of an underground tunneling vehicle. It was a large exhibit, as most of the ones were in the Museum of Transportation. It was a very old item, which had become fragile with age. The glass case around it protected it as much from the elements as from curious fingers. As she came to a stop beside the marble base. A loud bang was followed by the glass casing exploding above her. Tiny pieces of the glass rained down on and around her. She looked at chunks of the glass and was glad it was a safety type which didn't create sharp pieces.

By the time John swung the gun back to warn off any other do-gooders, she was standing off to his left, near an exhibit on air travel. She stood, unmoving, holding her breath. She did not want to attract his attention. Not yet, anyway.

John started back toward the group by the bench and found the four elders blocking his line of sight.

When he was about six feet away from them, he stopped. He once again held his right wrist and pointed the gun at the head of the tallest of the elders.

"Move," he growled. "I have to end him – third time's a charm, ain't it?"

The Fourth took one step forward, his red robes barely moving.

John shook his head just a little from side to side. A natural, simple motion which should have saved him.

"No, move *away* from that impostor. I've never failed to close a contract. One hundred contracts without fail. Except one, except my fir…" He stopped in mid-sentence. He swung the gun as quick as he could toward what he had glimpsed when he shook his head. A blur with red hair had been barreling down on him.

Even though he must have been over sixty, and obviously walking with a limp, he should have still been able to get off a shot at her before she closed the gap…except he hesitated. Another movement caught his eye and drew his attention. Leo had finally gotten a strong hold of Santore Noss, and sent him flying into the back of the four elder's legs. Three of them toppled over like bowling pins, the Fourth, because he was a little more forward, had his heels clipped and fell backward. That, coupled with Leo yelling "NO," slowed down John's reaction time just a hair.

But it was enough.

Imrial swung the staff she had taken from Santore Noss in mid-run, not taking the time to slow down. The head of the staff shattered on John's left arm, breaking his elbow. Imrial thought it was unfortunate that she had to attack from his left. It was his blind spot because the guards had distracted him from his right, but the gun was in his right hand. It would have been much better if she had been able to come from the other side.

John let out a low, guttural yell of pain. He instinctively dropped to his right knee, finishing his turn toward Imrial. When she hit his elbow, he let go of his right wrist, but not before he had dragged it down a little with the force of the blow. He brought the gun back up toward Imrial, keeping the hand near his chest so she couldn't get a swipe at the gun. She was making this very difficult. He meant to shoot her in the stomach, so the shot would go up into her chest. He wanted her to die slowly. He had become very skilled with guns, and at killing.

She didn't give him the chance.

When she smashed his elbow, the force of the blow jarred her arms, but she ignored that and concentrated on her footwork. She planted her right foot (her lead foot) firmly and let her momentum carry her into the air. She spun around, around John, and landed with a thud behind him and to his right, just as he raised the gun to where she had been when she struck him.

With two hands she swung what was left of the staff into the right side of his head. It made a loud *swuck* sound.

It was quick, very quick.

No gasp of surprise. He made no sound at all. He crumpled to the floor unconscious.

Imrial turned to assess the overall damage John had

done.   One guard was down, nose broken, pride wounded.   She turned to Leo and saw six bodies sprawled on the floor in front of the bench where Jenny was coming around.   The Fifth Elder was rubbing Jenny's hand.

Leo was the first to gain his feet.

He looked over toward Imrial.   She was panting lightly from the exertion.   The adrenaline burst was wearing off.   He looked at her with mixed emotions – first anger that she had taken out John before he could, then admiration for the same, and finally a little disappointment.

She watched his face change, and wondered at the last emotion that fixed on his face.

He looked at her wrist, the wrist which only moments before seemed broken, keeping her from helping the unconscious Genevieve.

Imrial looked at her wrist, too.   Then she gave him an "oops" shrug, smiled, and started giving orders to the guards.

He couldn't help but smile back.   She was amazing.

Once the rest gained their feet and composure, Santore Noss began a prepared speech.

"Leonard Hardy, Son of . . ."

"Later.   First we get everyone to the castle of Nahasar," the Fifth announced.   "No more surprises."

Three guards were securing John's hands.

Another stood over the gun looking very serious.   He knew not to touch it, someone else, like the Captain of the Guard, would know what to do with it.

Four of the guards ushered Leo, Santore, the Elder Five, Imrial and Genevieve to the docks.   Only Imrial spoke as they made their way through the island.   She had taken one of the guard's communication devices and was speaking with the Captain of the Guard.   She switched the frequency and told the pilot they were on their way. A large hovership was waiting for them, just offshore.

Imrial turned off the device and turned to the Fifth Elder. "Why not stay here? Isn't the island secure?" Imrial asked.

"Not really. The island is totally open, with only the museum security guards to provide protection. Until Leonard is crowned king, he is at risk," the Fifth answered, "and on Nahasar the elite guard has the castle secure."

"But, there's a lot I have to tell you," Imrial said.

"Good. We have a lot of questions, but we'll have time on Nahasar, away from so many ears." The Fifth raised his hand in greeting to the pilot of the hovership.

The hovership was a large transport craft. The main room was impressive, with a ceiling fourteen feet above the floor. The width of the cabin was twenty-eight and a half feet in the middle, tapering off to fifteen feet at each end. It had the shape of a large beetle, its metal hull gleamed a dark blue in the warm sun. The ramp extended from the rear of the ship. Eight legs, four from each side, protruded out and down. Jets of clean air shot from each. After they entered the craft, the ramp drew up and into the ship. The back lifted to close the opening, and two sets of wings extended away from the hull of the ship out into the air. The wingspan, including the body, was over seventy-five feet. The streams of air increased until the ship rose fifty feet off the water and they began the trip to Nahasar.

Is Clean Energy possible? When energy is dispersed through the use of fuel, there must be the creation of waste or residue from the process. It was believed that renewable and non-renewable energy were the two main types of energy. A non-renewable energy resource would include all sources of fuel which have a finite level of availability. Coal, nuclear and oil are examples of finite and therefore non-renewable resources. Each also produces a harmful byproduct when they are turned into energy. Wood was proposed as a renewable resource, since trees can be planted, but the amount of fertile soil to produce the trees is limited. Also, trees are not a readily (quickly) replenished resource and they also produce a harmful byproduct on consumption - therefore trees are not a viable choice. It was believed that wind and solar energy as fuels were renewable, continuously available and of infinite replenishment. We now know that this is false. These natural sources of energy are not guaranteed. The question is, can we have clean energy? The renewable resources have the benefit of offering a harnessing of energy that already exists (not being created by consumption of non-renewable resources) and therefore clean. Can we create a more predictable source of energy which would have the same properties? Sunlight, sun heat, and wind are all natural, and they also are all non-pollutants. They work in concert with our planet's ecosystem, as a necessary and useful collaborator. Can we find a comparable source of energy which can be controlled?

> - "The Challenge, An End Without A
>   Means" excerpt from a speech
>   given by John F. Recorn, Minister
>   of Energy, Barbados, to the
>   Conference on World Energy,
>   May, 2010.

9

"…and you will be escorted…"

When they reached the palace, Santore Noss was explaining the schedule for the coronation. He continued all the way from the main entrance to the inner entrance -- a massive oak, two-door affair. The doors were at least 2 stories high.

"…bow. Not you of course, but…"

The building looked like it was made from a type of brick. It resonated power and charm all at once. Leo barely got the chance to take it in before he was rushed inside and up the main stairs. Grans and he walked arm-in-arm, with Imrial in front, and Santore Noss behind still going over the details.

"…then I'll…"

Guards led the way and followed, always within five feet in front and five feet in back. The entourage ended up at the King's Suite. The guards flanked the doorway and Grans and Leo walked in. Imrial turned to stop Santore at the entrance to the room.

"…when the music…"

"Enough," Imrial said. She not only said it, but demonstrated her seriousness by putting her hand in the middle of Santore Noss' chest and giving a soft push. He took two steps back, a questioning look on his face.

"…tilted slightly, ever so slightly, to the…"

Imrial closed the door in his face.

"Grans, wha…" Leo started to ask. She put a finger on her lips, and led him over to a couch. The room was impressive. It was a large suite, with three attached rooms. He could make out an enormous, four-poster bed in one room. The doors to the other rooms were closed. The main room of the suite had an ornate couch, a set of large, uncomfortable-looking chairs, and a low coffee table. The table had a big bouquet of flowers in the middle. A beautiful, roll-top desk adorned one wall, a fireplace took up the opposite wall, and to his right were three floor-to-ceiling windows opening onto a balcony. A large chandelier hung from the 20-foot high ceiling.

Leo found it all quite impressive.

He sat down as instructed, silent as requested. He watched as Imrial checked every nook, cranny, and corner in the suite. Leo got a peek at the other two rooms when she opened the door to enter and exit them. One was another bedroom, with a much smaller bed and a small desk. It had bright white walls, brighter than he had ever seen before. The furniture was all a light sepia-tone wood. The upholstery and bedding were a deep maroon. The other room was a private bath. All he could see of that one was that it was also bright white, with softer, off-white furnishings, so that couldn't make out one item from the next. When she finished with the adjacent rooms, she came back and gave the same thorough examination of the main room.

Leo liked the main room. The walls were a calming shade of pastel blue. But the room didn't seem to calm Imrial down, she was non-stop motion. She even started looking under furniture. It was as if she had lost an earring or something – at least until she started looking along walls, drapes, and under lampshades.

After a long fifteen minutes, she came over and sat in a chair to their right.

"Clear," she said, sighing. She flopped on the chair, both feet out in front of her, legs spread, and let her head hang forward on her chest. "What a day."

Leo would have laughed at how she flopped on the chair, if he wasn't so tired himself. It had been a very, very, long day.

"OK, so what's going on?" Leo asked.

"Well, they think you're your grandfather. And I guess they think I'm someone who got dragged along by accident. Obviously a friend of yours," Grans offered.

"Can they be that dumb?" Imrial asked the question before Leo could.

No one had spoken on the trip from the museum to Nahasar except Santore Noss. He wouldn't stop talking. He described, in detail, all of the preparations he had made for the coronation - from the ordering of flowers, to the menu for the reception. He seemed more like a wedding planner than a chief advisor to a king. Even if the Elder Five had wanted to quiz Leo, they never got the chance to, which all involved, agreed was a good thing.

"No, they're not dumb." Jenny looked at Imrial. "They just don't fully understand time travel."

"I'm not buying it," Leo said. "Didn't you say those old guys…?"

"The Elder Five," Imrial corrected him.

"The Elder Five…figured out how to send you after Gramps? If they could figure that out, they must be smart enough to know I'm not him."

They thought about it for a while.

"I think they must know," Grans finally offered.

"Duh," Leo added.

"And who you are?" Imrial asked Grans, a little nervous.

"They may know that I'm Genevieve, but they have no way of knowing that I'm actually Leo's grandmother!" Just then, it sunk in. That made her the matriarch of Nahasar.

"I don't think they know who you are at all," Imrial said. She was shaking her head. "They're wise, but nearsighted. They barely recognized *me*!"

At that, they all laughed. She was right, the old guys didn't seem to see or recognize anything except that their precious King had returned, albeit a little younger than when he left.

"And what do you think they'll make of John?"

"What was all those things he was saying?" Imrial asked.

"I'm guessing he spent a lot of time watching movies," Genevieve said.

"But what was that about the 'third time being a charm'?" Imrial asked.

"Probably just mixed up the saying. That was only the second time he's tried to kill me, right?" Leo said.

They sat thinking about it for a little while.

"But he was so old."

And they thought some more.

"I think they have too much on their minds right now to worry about anything except getting Leo installed as king. Nahasar needs a king. They need Leo to bring stability to the country," Grans said seriously.

"But if the Elder Five know…" he began.

"They know you're not the Leonard Hardy that left. They also know you must be his descendant since we were targeted on your DNA. But, they need a Hardy," Grans explained.

"So, what am I supposed to do? I can't pass myself off as Gramps – I still have trouble understanding them, especially if they speak fast." Leo couldn't help thinking of Santore Noss, whose singsong, non-stop talk kept making him feel sleepy.

"Just nod a lot. I will whisper in your ear and Immy will make sure you don't have to field too many questions," Grans said.

"Immy?" Leo looked at Imrial.

"Wipe that smile off your face," Imrial said.

This made his grin actually broaden into a full-fledged smile.

"So just nod a lot?"

"Yes." Grans said.

"Great. I'll look like an idiot."

"Only if you keep smiling like that" Imrial said.

"No, you'll come across as thoughtful, wise, and willing to accept counsel," Grans offered. They laughed again.

"Anyway," Grans added, "you'll have it down pat by the time of the coronation."

Someone knocked on the door. Before anyone could answer it, the door swung open.

Leo guessed he knew how fast Imrial was from what happened in the museum, but he hadn't actually seen her in action. He was trying to get out from under Santore Noss at the time. Grans and Leo had enough time to look toward the door at the sound of the knock. Leo even entertained speaking, but before he could, Imrial had leapt up from her seemingly exhausted position on the chair and was at the door. A woman pushed in a cart with three shelves. Each shelf had silver covered dishes. She didn't seem to notice Imrial standing by the door. She definitely didn't notice that Imrial's body was taut, pulled tight like a bow, ready to release an arrow.

Slowly, Imrial relaxed.

"Your meal, Sire," the woman said as she bowed.

"You can leave it. I'll serve," Imrial told her. The woman bowed again, stole a peek in Leo's direction, and hurried out. The guard closed the door behind her.

"I'm not worried about his speech, I'm worried about how he acts," Imrial said, not missing a beat from their conversation. She wheeled the cart over to the coffee table and started removing plates.

"Nothing to worry about there," Grans offered. "His

grandfather was a janitor! He hated ceremony, and would actually fight having to learn any etiquette." She turned to Leo. "Just be yourself. You have it in you to be a great ruler, you just don't know it yet."

She smiled at him, a grandmother's smile, full of pride and hope.

Leo smiled back, a scared boy's smile, full of anxiety and fear.

It was going to be an interesting life...definitely interesting.

Grans and Imrial kept to their word. They rarely let Leo out of their sight. Partly to protect him, but mostly to keep anyone from finding out that he wasn't Leonard Hardy. They had been right, he looked the part well enough to get by. Little by little, his accent faded, as did Jenny's. They were worried about Leo's accent, since no one seemed to know how long Leonard Hardy had been gone, but since he was so young, they assumed it wasn't long enough to pick up an accent. No one seemed to recognize Jenny. The most popular rumor was that she was an accidental passenger on Imrial's return trip. Imrial and Grans did not correct their misconceptions.

Elonce was a world predominantly covered by water. Land masses accounted for only 25% of the surface of the planet. It was a clean planet. The water teemed with life, the land was covered in green, vibrant foliage. On Elonce, there was a balance between human needs, and the needs of the planet. They were not at odds.

Nahasar was one of the best examples of this balance. Nothing was wasted. No byproducts polluted the land, sea, or skies. All energy was produced cleanly. It wasn't that amazing, really, but Leo Hardy, the soon-to-be-crowned King of Nahasar, was speechless. He stood on one of the many balconies in the palace, leaning on the massive stone railings. What a strange structure the palace was. It had an almost equal mix of wood, marble, stone, and brick. He breathed in the fresh air.

Nahasar was one of the five nations of Elonce. It was also the name of the continent. A continent that Leo found himself at the head of, but it wasn't the kingship that had him in shock – it was the condition of his country. "My country" sounded strange, but also somehow natural to him. It was a beautiful place. He couldn't stop marveling over the lack of pollution. The rich, blue skies, the plants greener, than anything he'd ever seen, the people – so healthy looking. Definitely an oxygen rich environment. The colors almost seemed unreal. Grey, as a color, didn't seem to exist. Everything was bright and vibrant.

"How does it work?" Leo asked.

"How does what work?" the Second Elder asked.

"Why isn't there any pollution?" Leo still couldn't tell Elders apart. He had been in the castle for two days now, and rather than having questions answered, he was more confused than ever. That, and the complication that everyone thought he was his grandfather, made it harder for him to ask what he wanted to know.

"It's very simple, really."

"Then explain it to me," Leo said.

"Well, the explanation isn't simple."

Typical double-talk. It was all he ever got out of Santore Noss, so he was getting used to it.

"Why the sudden interest in the mechanics of energy production?" the Second Elder asked. Leo wished he knew which one he was talking to.

"I saw some interesting things on Earth, so I'm curious why we're so different," Leo said, not lying.

"Different time, different place," was all the Elder would say. He understood that saying…he had heard it enough times. The Elder bowed and took his leave of Leo, probably tired of his silly questions. He had become comfortable with their speech. He could understand them pretty easily now. The same couldn't be said for them understanding Leo. A lifetime of using slang didn't help his cause, and he knew he was mispronouncing some words.

The coronation would be in two more days, and Leo still wasn't sure if it was the right thing to do. Grans and Imrial insisted that keeping his identity secret was the only responsible thing to do. And if the Elder Five knew and were keeping it secret, maybe it was. Nahasar needed a king, and obviously it was meant to be Leo.

At least that's how the three of them rationalized it.

Sometimes Leo had doubts. He stood, leaning on the balcony railing. The view was spectacular and he found himself spending most of his time on one balcony or another, breathing in the air. As of yet, they wouldn't let him set foot outside the castle. He guessed that once he was King they couldn't tell him what to do, but until then, he didn't have much power. He took another deep breath of what had to be the cleanest air he had ever tasted. It was refreshing, like a cold glass of clear, mountain water. Leo guessed it felt so good because it had a large amount of oxygen and almost no pollutants. It amazed him every time he breathed it in. It must have been what the air was like on Earth, before the industrial revolution.

The colors in the sky were amazing, too. The blues were so blue…Leo had never seen a sky so blue, except in movies. Sometimes that's what it all felt like - like he was in a movie. The only thing missing was a soundtrack. Just then, he noticed there *was* a soundtrack. Soft, but definite, in the background. Leo walked back into the great hall from the balcony, following the sound.

The Great Hall was, well...great. It had cathedral ceilings, marble pillars spaced out every fifty feet or so, and a remarkable wood parquet floor. Everything had been washed, waxed, and dusted for the coronation. At present, there were no tables or chairs in the hall. Leo figured they were out being cleaned, too. It usually took him over five minutes to cross the hall from one end to the other. Partly because of its immense size, but also because he liked to examine the hanging tapestries. He could spend the whole day looking at them. They were amazing works, hand woven. They depicted the history of Nahasar, from the end of the Last War to now.

"Last War" because that's what it was. Leo thought about the "war to end all wars" he had read about in history class. How it wasn't even close to the truth. There had been wars almost non-stop ever since. But Elonce seemed to have found true, global peace. And based on the tapestry, the "last war" was a long, long time ago.

Leo never wanted to be caught staring, as he didn't know if it would arouse suspicion, so he just walked as slowly as he could, as if in thought, down one side of the hall and then the other. Once, he stopped to examine a scene on the tapestry hanging near the East entrance. A servant approached him almost immediately.

"May I help you, Sire?" an elderly lady, dressed in light blue with a white apron, asked.

Leo almost laughed.

"No, I'm fine," he said, still looking at the tapestry.

"I can have it cleaned again," she said.

"No, I...it's fine," he said and continued his walk to the balcony. That was when he realized making believe he was his grandfather was a bad idea.

His grandfather hadn't been royalty, in fact, he was a janitor at the museum of transportation, but there were still so many things people expected him to know. Simple stuff, like what he wanted to eat. How would he know what they had? He could make out what most people said now, but he didn't want to try to have any long, or in-depth, conversations. Thankfully, for the most part, everyone steered clear of him.

Probably worried he'd want something.

Or that he'd ask another stupid question.

It became clear that first day that Imrial didn't need to run interference for him half as much as she thought.

The music was clearer here. Leo headed down one of the corridors leading off the Great Hall, following it. It was getting louder. If an ominous bass drum or a screeching violin had started, he would have swung around to see what evil was approaching from behind. He had to laugh at himself. When he did, the music paused. Then it started again, quieter than before. He found the door where the music was coming from and knocked. He kept forgetting that as the future king, he didn't need to knock.

"Come in," a voice called out.

Leo opened the door and stepped into a small room. It wasn't a bedroom, but then again it wasn't an office either. It had a small cot, a dresser, a table with writing utensils and paper, and a chair. The chair was pushed away from the table and a boy, a little younger than Leo, was sitting in it. He was playing what looked like a cross between a violin and a harmonica. When he saw Leo, he literally jumped out of the chair, knocking it over and smacking his knee on the bed's footboard.

"Sire?" he said through clenched teeth. Out of politeness, Leo ignored his discomfort.

"Sorry. Just curious who was playing," he said.

The boy tossed his instrument on the bed and bent down on one knee (his good one). He placed both hands over the knee he had banged, and lowered his head.

"Forgive me, Sire."

Leo wanted to laugh at his cleverness. He could barely make out that he was rubbing the spot where he smacked his knee.

The boy kept his head bowed. "I'll be playing with the orchestra at the coronation and I wanted to practice."

"Well, keep up the good work...er"

"Sean, Sire. Sean Bulthoware. I work for Young Philip."

Leo had no clue who Young Philip was, but he didn't want to keep the boy from taking care of his bruise any longer than necessary.

"Nice to meet you," Leo said, immediately knowing it was the wrong thing for a king to say. He backed out of the room. He closed the door and headed back up the corridor to the great hall. Awkward encounters like that happened all the time.

Leo wanted to stop pretending. He hated making believe he was someone he wasn't. If the Elder Five knew he wasn't Leonard Hardy (which no one had confirmed for him yet), then why couldn't everyone know? He decided to ask one of the old guys next time he saw one. If they really knew he wasn't Leonard Hardy, then he'd get them to tell everyone. If they didn't know...well, he hoped the surprise wouldn't give them a heart attack or something.

"What's wrong, Leo?" Grans asked when he returned to the suite.

"I don't like this lying."

"I know, it's in direct opposition to your talent." Leo thought about it. He had never actually lied, but even avoiding the truth bothered him.

"I've decided to tell the next of the Elder Five I see."

"I know."

"I'm serious," Leo said, ready for a fight.

"I know," she said again.

"And?" his hands clenched into fists.

"And what? You've made up your mind, and I'll stand by you. You're going to be the next King of Nahasar, so I have to get used to you getting your way." She smiled.

"Really?" He took a breath. He hadn't realized he wasn't breathing.

"Sure. I think they already know anyway. And if they don't, it's probably better to get it out in the open before the coronation."

"But I thought you…"

"I didn't want whoever is after the throne to have an argument against you being crowned. But, I've been thinking about it. If we crown you under false pretenses, they may have a stronger argument to have you executed as an impostor."

"Thanks, I think." He was actually relieved.

Imrial flowed into the suite like a speedboat, bringing two guards in her wake. Grans stood up. They could both tell something was wrong.

"We've gotten intelligence that another attempt on your life is imminent," she said.

"When?" Leo asked

"Before dawn tomorrow."

"That's still cutting it close, the coronation is only two nights away," Grans calculated.

"We've been expecting it since we arrived in Nahasar, but we weren't sure of the type of attack," Imrial explained.

"And, what did you learn?" Leo asked.

"It's an inside job. The assassin is already in the palace. Which means it could be anyone."

"Where are the Elder Five?" he asked. The

realization that another attempt on his life was forthcoming made him want to tell the truth sooner.

"They went off to consult the Oracles. They said they'd be back at dinner time tomorrow…or at least one of them would be." Imrial answered. She positioned the two guards and checked the windows.

Leo wasn't sure why she was worried about someone coming in the windows – they were over 20 feet up. When it came to this world, he knew there was a lot he still didn't know.

"You said the threat was from inside," Leo said.

"Yes, at least that's the one we have intel on. I doubt they'd leave your death in one person's hands. They're getting desperate. If you're crowned king, they wouldn't dare touch you."

"I'm glad to hear it, but I still don't understand. Why would they give up once I was crowned king?"

Grans offered an explanation.

"It's a culture thing really. Once you're crowned king, you're the official ruler of one of the five nations of Elonce. If anyone were to harm you, they'd be hunted down, no matter what it took. It would be an affront to the whole world. On the other hand, if you're just a candidate for the throne, no one would look too hard to see who was behind it. It would cause too much trouble and turmoil. As long as you're killed discreetly, it'll be accepted."

"Accepted by who?"

"The other nations of course," Imrial answered.

"But if I'm the king…" Leo liked the idea of being king better now.

"They would be risking too much. They'd be hunted down and killed."

"Still…" Leo started to protest.

"And everyone in their family would also be killed."

He stopped his pacing. "What?"

"Everyone. Children, grandchildren, parents, grandparents, cousins, brothers, sisters, even pets. Their name would be erased from every book on Elonce."

"So why not crown me now?" Leo asked.

"It's not that simple," Grans said.

"Why not?"

"Ceremony is very important to our people."

Leo nodded at this.

"Also, you can't appear to be scared or ambitious," Imrial pointed out.

"I'm going to be king," he said. "How can I *not* look ambitious?"

"By not rushing the ceremony," Grans repeated. She didn't look disappointed that he hadn't figured out the obvious – probably because she realized he *had* figured it out. Leo fully understood, but couldn't help asking the questions. He wasn't used to just accepting things, he needed to hear someone confirm his deductions. She closed her eyes as if exhausted from the conversation. So, Leo stopped asking questions.

He headed toward the door instead.

"Where are you going?" Imrial almost barked at him. She was searching the walk-in wardrobe for the third time.

"I think I'll check on the preparations for tomorrow's dinner. Aren't we having guests?" Not a lie. Leo fully planned on checking them before he left the palace.

"What part of someone from inside the palace may try to kill you before tomorrow are you having trouble with?" she asked.

Grans stood up. She ignored Imrial's outburst and answered his question. "Yes, Santore Noss will have the guest list. It'll include at least one of the Elder Five, and I believe a representative from each of the other four nations." She walked over to Leo and put her arm through his. "I'll go with you."

"What is wrong with you two?" Imrial said, as she started to signal the guards to cut off their escape.

"Nothing. I believe you were the one who said I couldn't look afraid or ambitious." Leo hoped his shaking wasn't obvious. Grans must have noticed because she gave him a peck on the cheek. As she rose up to kiss him, she also pinched his arm with a wicked twist.

Leo held in a yell and shot her an angry glance.

"Better," she said, and he knew she meant anger was a better emotion to show than fear and he *was* angry. Not at the pinch…he didn't like being a target. He didn't like pretending he was someone he wasn't.

He didn't like waiting.

So, he let his anger show instead of his nervousness.

Imrial changed her orders from stopping them to escorting them.

Hereby signed by all five nations of Elonce with notarization by the Elder Five.

From this day forward, no machines of travel, production, or entertainment will emit pollutants of any kind. All existing machines that emit pollutants will heretofore be dismantled and their components recycled. It is the express belief of this congress that science has progressed to a point in space, time, and knowledge that allows it to create alternatives that emit no pollutants.

From this day forward, no act or behavior will be accepted that leads to pollution of the land, sea, air or space. Pollution is hereby outlawed as a crime against humanity and will not be tolerated. Specific examples of violations and their suggested penalties follow.

- Preamble of the Clean Air Act of Elonce

10

It was easier than he thought it would be.

After reviewing the preparations with Philia Salt (the head chef), Corliss Pfister (the lead wait staff), Angela Creshy (the orchestra conductor), and Kelly Pontoon (Santore Noss' assistant), Leo told Grans and Imrial that he was going to use the men's room. It was the oldest trick in the book, and he was surprised how easily they fell for it. Then again, he wasn't lying and they knew he couldn't lie.

Leo had found out on his first day in the palace that the bathroom had a dumbwaiter that went to common use bathrooms on each floor. He easily folded into the dumbwaiter and pressed the button for the basement. From there, he had no problems leaving through the service doorway. No resistance from the inside of the palace – the doors were locked to keep people out, not in.

When Leo opened the door onto the back lawn, the sun blinded him for a moment. It was a beautiful day – as every day of his stay on Elonce had been. He shielded his eyes with his arm, until they adjusted to the brightness.

There were two guards bowing to him.

"Please resume your duties." Leo had gotten much better at the kingly stuff.

"Yes, Sire," they said in unison, and took up their posts by the door.

Leo looked around, but didn't know how to get anywhere.

"Where can I find a ship to take me to Museum Island?"

"Sire," the guard bowed deeply again. "Follow the path to your right and you will find the garage. Young Philip will be there, and he can help you."

"Thank you," Leo said. The guard stood erect again. He was doing a poor job of hiding a smile under his stern military stare. It was the 'thank you.' Leo knew that most rulers didn't have time for pleasantries and rarely spoke directly to the help. Well, some things were definitely going to change when he became king.

"Have a good day," Leo added as he started off. He knew this would solicit even more chuckles and smiles, but he figured it was the least he could do. When Imrial found out that they let him stroll off on his own, she'd chew them up. They meant well. They'd probably remember in an hour or so that Imrial wanted to know about his whereabouts at all times – especially if he were seen alone.

Oh, well.

Leo found Young Philip working on one of the three hover-beetle thingy's. His legs were sticking out from underneath the rear-end of the craft.

"Excuse me…"

"One sec. My hands are full." He growled more than said. His voice was very deep, and pleasant, and slow. It reminded Leo of a movie star, he just couldn't remember the name.

When he crawled out from beneath the craft, Leo wondered at why they called him "Young Philip." He was easily 70 years old. He stood up and straightened his back with a loud creak and pop.

"Ahhh," he sighed, then started chewing on something. He reminded Leo of ball players working a chunk of chewing gum, shifting it from one side of his mouth to the other.

Leo wished Young Philip would hurry. Leo waited with more patience than he actually felt. It wouldn't be long before Imrial was escorting him back to his 'prison' if he didn't get moving.

"How can I help ya'?" He didn't seem to recognize Leo. Leo wasn't sure if this was good or bad.

"I need to go to Museum Island."

"Hmmm. Why'd that be, may I ask?" Even in his semi-bent-over state, he was a good 7 inches taller than Leo. He wiped his hands on a rag, although there wasn't a spot of grease or dirt anywhere.

"I'd like to see the Curator."

"That makes sense. I guess you have some questions for him, eh?" He smiled at Leo. Leo realized he did recognize him. Even so, Young Phillip treated him like a commoner. Again, Leo wondered if this was good or bad.

"Well, you can take the blue one. It's fully prepped."

"Thanks." Leo said, but didn't move. He just looked

at the large, blue, beetle-like hovercraft.

"I guess you'll be wanting a pilot, too?" Young Philip asked.

Leo looked at him, and to no surprise found he was smiling from ear to ear. His creased face was old, but strong. His skin was very dark and tight like leather. He smiled even wider.

Leo realized this man was having fun at his expense!

Leo refused to oblige him with an answer.

Young Philip broke out into a loud laugh. His laughter was so strong and spontaneous that whatever he was chewing on flew out of his mouth and landed near Leo's foot.

Philip doubled over, laughing louder and louder. Finally, when he got control of himself, he looked up at Leo.

"Thorry," he said, his speech garbled.

Young Philip walked over to Leo, and bowed lower than anyone had since Leo had arrived. Leo thought to himself, "Finally, some respect."

"Darn things," Young Phillip said as he picked up his false teeth from beside Leo's foot and put them back in his mouth. So much for respect. He straightened up and looked down at Leo.

"Now, Sire, you know you're not supposed to be walking about the grounds alone. And there's no way I can let you have a flyer. Are you trying to get Young Philip killed?"

"No," Leo said, sullenly and honestly.

To have come so close to escaping, just to be turned away by a 70 year-old giant was hard to swallow.

"Why didn't, why don't you…" Leo tried feebly.

"Why don't I treat you like a king? Well, first of all, you're not king yet. That's another couple of days away."

Leo had to smile. All this time, he hadn't wanted to

be treated special, and the first time someone treated him like a normal person, he had been offended.

"And secondly, you're not Leonard Hardy...so I'm waiting to see if you actually get crowned or executed before I waste any effort in bowing to you." Young Philip's smile left.

Leo stared at him. He knew? Leo knew it wasn't due to Imrial or Jenny letting it slip - they were too disciplined for that. No, somehow this old man was wiser than everyone he had met so far. Leo decided to wait him out. If Leo had learned anything from Grans, it was that many times, silence was the best response.

"I knew Leonard. Good kid. I got him his job at the Museum," Young Philip said.

Now it was Leo's turn to smile.

"Was friends with his parents," Young Philip stated with finality. It was his turn to wait Leo out.

They stood in silence for a while, until Leo deduced where he needed to go.

"I'm not an impostor, and I would never harm any of the Hardy's." That elicited the response he hoped for. The old giant relaxed, the tenseness leaving his shoulders and face. Leo had thought he could be an assassin, and Young Philip had been equally wrong in his thought that Leo had hurt Leonard and replaced him. Funny how people always imagine the worst.

"I'm his grandson, Leo Hardy"

The giant bent closer to Leo's face. He looked him over carefully. Then he leaned even closer and looked Leo over again. He stared into Leo's eyes and then a genuine smile creased his face. His breath smelled of peppermint and his eyes shone.

"How?" he asked.

"Time travel."

He nodded, not because he knew what Leo meant,

but because he understood the story would take more time than Leo had available.

"He was only a little older than you, last I saw him." He rubbed his chin. "Is he happy?"

This old 'Young Philip' was the only person on this planet that seemed to care if Leonard Hardy was happy.

Leo looked down.

"He's dead. He died after a full life, and I believe he is very happy." Young Philip just bowed his head. "I'm here to fulfill his last wish," Leo added.

After a moment, the giant lifted his face again, smiled and grabbed Leo's arms in his large hands.

"Hot chili in the middle of winter! You really are his grandson, aren't you?"

Leo couldn't help but smile back at him.

"Yes, and I need to see the Curator." He didn't want to be so abrupt, but he felt strongly that he had to get on his way if he were going to make it.

"Yes, I agree. But I still can't let you go without permission, or a pilot." Young Philip let go of Leo and started back to his work.

"But…"

"No fear, Ms. Imrial will take you. She's a pilot, you know," he said.

"No. I mean, I didn't know that, but, well, she doesn't know I'm going."

He bent down, grabbed onto a wing of the craft, and lowered himself to the ground. "She does now," he gave a nod, letting Leo know that she was standing behind him. He slid back under the belly and started banging something softly.

"I thought you couldn't lie," she said.

Leo turned, expecting a full escort, but she was alone. She looked radiant – her hair was pulled back in a ponytail. She was wearing a leather-looking jacket, high boots, and a weapon on her hip. The weapon looked like a short sword or a long knife. Her pants were just a little more than tights. She held out a jacket for him.

Leo took it and put it on.

"I didn't lie. I just didn't tell you everything." Leo didn't tell her that even that small deception through omission made him feel ill.

"No more secrets," she said as she headed toward the blue flyer. "Philip, we'll be back by dinner."

Young Philip mumbled something.

She started checking the craft, in what Leo deduced was a pre-flight check.

"So, do you have a death wish?" She was baiting him, but he didn't mind.

"No. I want to see the Curator. I don't buy the 'everything will be OK once I'm crowned' story."

"Good. I don't either." Obviously honesty wasn't one of *her* talents.

"So, that's why you're helping me?" Leo asked.

"Partly. And partly because, as I'm sure you already figured out, if there is an assassin in the palace, the safest place for you is somewhere else."

Leo smiled. That was going to be his argument if he got caught. He jogged back over to where Young Philip was working.

"Philip?" Leo had a thought, an intuition. He wasn't sure it was based on deduction, but he knew it was due to one of his talents.

"Yes, Sire?" Leo knew Young Philip was smiling even though he couldn't see his face from his position under the ship.

"You have a young man working with you, Sean Bul…" Leo began.

"Sean Bulthoware," Young Philip finished for him.

Imrial walked around to the other side of the craft,

still doing her check.

"Yes, how long has Sean been working here?"

"A couple of weeks. I don't know if you'd call it working though, the kid's as lazy as they come. He'd rather join in the gossip than do his work."

"How long has he been in the orchestra?"

"The royal orchestra? Never. I mean, he's not. Not that I know of."

"Where is he now?" Leo asked almost in a whisper. He didn't want Imrial to hear the answer, he wanted to see the Curator.

"He's supposed to be sick in his room." Young Philip understood. He slid out from under the craft. "I'll make sure I check up on him."

Leo hoped that his expression showed his concern.

"Ready to go?" Imrial called from behind him.

Leo smiled and turned.

"I can't wait," he called back to her.

Leo sat in the co-pilot's chair, the large transport eerily empty. Leo thought for a moment that maybe it would be better if they took some guards with them after all.

"Buckle up," she ordered.

Leo did as he was told. She pulled the craft out of the garage smoothly. They rose up over the West wall and out across the countryside. Leo hadn't taken the time to observe the flight in, so this time he paid special attention. Nahasar was amazing. All the colors were rich and deep. Vibrant. Everything seemed alive.

"You may want to breathe," Imrial said.

Leo looked at her, confused, and then realized she was right. He had been holding his breath.

"Is that why they say something is 'breathtaking'?"

"Who says that?" She was busy working the instruments and maneuvering the craft.

"Never mind."

"Would you like to fly over the capitol?" she offered.

Leo could see a gleaming city in the distance. No smoke, no smog, just gleaming, shining structures.

"Is it on the way?" he asked.

"Not really," she said.

"Maybe next time. I want to get to the bottom of all this as soon as possible."

"In that case hold on. If you want to get there fast, I'll have to break a rule or two."

The flyer seemed to pause in mid-air and then turned north. A humming rose beneath their feet and then they were flying at roller coaster speed. Leo could barely make out anything in the foreground – it all blurred under the speed. Only items far off were clear and growing steadily. Leo figured they wouldn't be making a quiet, unnoticed arrival.

"So much for stealth," he said.

"Stealth is overrated" Imrial answered.

The Island of Museums was a marvel. The five museums were independent facilities on the island, but each fit perfectly with the others. Leo was sure that the same architect designed them all. The Museum of Transportation, the only one he had been in, albeit briefly, was a dome structure, like football stadiums on Earth. The only difference was, the dome was a clear, glass-like surface, which allowed for viewing of the displays from above, and viewing of the skies from within.

Leo noticed as they passed the Museum of Science that its five spires were also made of a transparent material. He could see the shapes of different displays hanging from the center of the spires, but couldn't make them out. They were still going a bit fast.

Imrial landed the craft at the docks, where all ships were required to park.

"Does everything come in fives on Elonce?" Leo asked as he unbuckled.

"No, some things come in threes." Again, that smile. Leo enjoyed it on the few occasions he could get one out of her.

Imrial was already outside before he finally got free of his harness. As he left the craft, he was glad for the jacket she had given him. Near the water, the wind was a lot cooler. Leo could hear someone speaking with Imrial, speaking quite forcefully.

"I'm very sorry Miss, but the Island is closed today. It's our cleaning day."

"I understand. We're not here to visit; we need to see the Curator…"

"I'm sorry."

Leo cleared the second wing of the beetle craft and stepped into the sunlight. It felt good on his face, compared to the cold air off the water.

"Look. Call your boss, and tell him…"

"Her," the guard corrected.

"Tell *her* we need to speak with the Curator. It's important."

"One moment then." The guard turned his head away from them and cupped his hand over his right ear. It looked like he was talking to himself, or maybe into a microphone hidden in his sleeve. Leo looked at the uniform. It was the same as all the museum guards, with the same sword at the waist on a very fancy belt. The only weapons Leo had seen on Elonce were these swords.

"Don't you have guns here?" he asked Imrial, whispering so as not to disturb the guard's conversation with his sleeve.

"No. There are no guns here. Except the one that John brought back from your world. We only have them in the museum of history. Well, maybe there's one or two in the Museum of Science too."

"And no one uses them?" Leo asked.

"No. They're dishonorable. Also, they're non-functioning. They've been disabled." She was watching the guard.

"Are swords the only weapon around here?" he asked.

"The only accepted weapon. They are very honorable. Also, most people won't use them...too messy, it discourages violence."

"The only accepted weapon? I seem to remember someone using a ceremonial staff."

"Flexibility is the cousin of innovation," she quoted.

"Don't you mean 'necessity is the mother of invention?'?" Leo asked. She gave him a quizzical look.

The guard saved Leo from having to explain, "Miss, you have clearance," he said, with a hint of disappointment.

"Thanks. Where can we find the Curator?" She was on the move again. Reflection was definitely not one of her talents.

"One moment." He went back to his sleeve.

Imrial, satisfied that they were going to be able to see the Curator, paused and turned her full attention to Leo again. This time Leo smiled.

"OK, so, no weapons of mass destruction here, eh?" he asked.

"Huh?"

"I mean, no missiles, machine guns, atom bombs, biological agents. Nothing to kill a lot of people at once? How are wars fought?"

"Hmm. There are things like what you describe in some of the museums, but for the most part – no. We have no weapons to destroy mass." Leo had to laugh.

"That's probably a good thing," he managed to get out through his laughing.

"I think so," she said seriously.

"So, why are you worried about a civil war in Nahasar? Wouldn't it just be a couple of people fighting with swords?"

"No. We don't have wars that way. If there were a civil war over the rule of Nahasar, the two factions would cease to communicate. There would be no travel, trading, sport or recreation. Nothing. The nation would be divided, and Nahasar would cease to be harmonious."

"Harmonious?" Leo was confused. It didn't seem like a big deal.

"Yes. Everything would stop and it would be a lousy place to live. Civil war would destroy our country."

It may have been the first time that Leo realized Imrial was from Nahasar. It hadn't dawned on him that when he became King, she'd be one of his subjects. Her bossy attitude and the way she was totally in charge, would have to change drastically. Leo smiled at this.

"It's not funny," she said, again very serious.

"No, it's not. You're right," was all he could manage without laughing again – which would not be good.

"He's in the Museum of Literature." The guard pointed up the hill.

"Thank you very much," Imrial said. She made it a point to bow to the guard, letting Leo know what politeness looked like. She was a little angry with him for laughing at her.

Leo bowed to the guard also. For a king, an inappropriate thing to do.

Of course, this just made her angrier.

"Let's go!" she grumbled.

The guard and Leo shared a smile, and Leo had to jog to catch up to her.

When they reached the Museum of Literature, another guard was there to meet them. She wore the same uniform as the one at the dock, but the color of the sash that went from her belt and over her left shoulder was red. All the other guards had a blue sash. At least, all the ones Leo had seen.

"Miss Imrial?" the guard asked. She had an air of importance about her. She also had blonde hair pulled back into a single, long ponytail.

"Yes. We're here to see the Curator," Imrial said. She didn't seem surprised that the guard knew her name. Leo began to wonder if Imrial was just a military agent of Nahasar, or if she was something more. He'd have to ponder this when he had more time.

"I'll take you to him." She turned and headed into the museum. Two doors slid apart as she approached.

Leo noticed that no one addressed him. They were all carefully avoiding recognizing him.

"So, my escape wasn't as secret as I thought?" Leo whispered to Imrial's back.

"Jenny predicted it."

They passed a few art exhibits, a sculpture, and a gallery of paintings. On Elonce, literature included art as well as writing. They passed at least three rooms which Leo would have called libraries. There were wall-to-wall, floor-to-ceiling books. More books than he had ever seen.

For a world so far more advanced than Earth in technology, it was strange seeing paper, canvas, and marble. Leo guessed that's why they were in a museum. He hesitated. Something tugged at his mind. The same intuitive feelings he had about Sean Bulthoware. Leo somehow knew there was an answer to at least one of his many questions in this room…he couldn't quite figure out what.

"Sir?" the guard called to him.

Leo looked up. Both she and Imrial were waiting at another door. He looked around. If only he had more time.

"Coming," Leo said, and joined them. They entered a hallway and went through another door and up two flights of stairs. The guard opened the door and waited for Leo and Imrial to go through.

"He's waiting for you," she said, closing the door behind them.

"Thanks," Leo said to the closed door. When he turned, Imrial had her hand up in a gesture telling him to wait. She was slightly crouched, as if she were going to pounce on something. She scanned the room.

"There is nothing to fear," a small voice said. It came from a child standing in front of them. Leo couldn't figure out how they hadn't seen him.

The boy turned and walked into the center of the room. Leo started to follow, but Imrial held him back, with a gentle hand on his arm.

"What?" Leo whispered.

"I don't know." She stared at the boy. "And, I don't like not knowing."

The boy was now in the center of the room. The only light came through the glass ceiling, but it lit the whole room quite well. Imrial was still scanning the room.

"It's alright," the boy said. Although he was at least fifty feet away, Leo heard him as clearly as when he was standing directly in front of them.

Leo looked down and noticed there was sand on the floor. Lots of sand. Colored sand.

"You won't ruin it," the boy said.

"We're here to see the Curator," Imrial yelled out, although the boy didn't seem to be yelling.

"Are you? Please come here."

Leo started to follow his instructions, and Imrial tried to hold him back again.

"It's alright," Leo whispered. "No pin pricks."

She followed him, still holding onto his arm.

Leo expected to feel the sand underfoot, but didn't. It was as if they were walking on a sheet of glass over the sand.

"You said you came to see the Curator…but that's not accurate," the boy said as they finally reached him.

"How is that not accurate?" Imrial said defensively. "We want to see him!"

The boy said nothing. He looked directly at Leo.

"Do you like it?"

"I can't quite make it out," Leo answered.

"True. You're too close to see it." With that, they all began to rise as if on an elevator. They went up slowly and smoothly. No problems with balance, no gust of wind. When they were about twenty feet above the floor they stopped.

"Beautiful," Leo said. The entire floor was covered with sand, making the largest sand painting he had ever seen. It was breathtaking. Later, when Jenny asked, Leo couldn't describe it, because he had nothing to relate it to. He knew it represented life, a picture of the essence of life, but he didn't know how he knew.

"Thank you," the boy said.

Imrial, thankfully, was speechless.

"So, why did you come here?" the boy asked Leo.

"To ask the Curator for help."

"That's still quite vague," he said. He was admiring the painting while looking Leo in the eye at the same time.

"To ask if he knew who wanted to kill me."

"Why would *he* know?" the boy asked.

"I heard he knows everything." Leo didn't say it sarcastically or with malice. It was what he had heard from one of the cooks, and she totally believed it, even if Leo didn't.

"Do you believe that?" It seemed that there were others on Elonce with the talent to read faces – or maybe the boy could read minds.

"My belief isn't important – only that he may know the answer."

"Or is it only important that he tell you the answer," the boy said, winning that round.

"Will you take us to the Curator?" Imrial had regained her voice.

"No."

"Does the Curator actually know all?" Leo asked.

"Yes."

"Will he tell us who is behind the assassination attempt?" Imrial asked. Leo knew the answer, but for once, she wasn't as quick as he was.

"No. He doesn't do that anymore," the boy said, confirming Leo's guess.

"Do what?" she asked.

"Give people what they ask for. He used to do that, but then people stopped growing and learning."

"But if he knows all, he could stop bad things from happening; murders, crime, accidents…" Imrial was just getting started.

"He could stop the act, but not the intent. He couldn't make someone not want to do evil, just take away the opportunity. Hence the lack of growth. Without pain, there is no change, without sorrow there is no regret."

"But why allow so *much* pain – he could at least stop

wars and catastrophes!" she pressed.

"Yes. So he did."

Imrial stopped arguing. Leo could see her thinking it through. From what he had learned since arriving on Elonce, there hadn't been a catastrophe or war in centuries.

"Is that why there are Oracles?" Leo asked.

"Yes," he said.

"Do you know who is trying to kill me?" Leo pressed.

"I know much more than that." The boy looked at Leo and smiled. "Do you believe me?"

"Yes," Leo said without thinking about it.

"I'm sorry, but the answer you seek is not mine to tell." They began to slowly descend toward the floor. This answer was very familiar. It sounded like Grans telling him it wasn't her story to tell.

"So, what is it that you *can* tell me?"

Leo was catching on.

"Find Henders, one of the Historians, for the answers you seek."

They stopped a few inches above the floor. Leo hadn't realized it when they walked into the room, but they were always at least a few inches off the floor.

"Thank you," Leo said.

"You're very welcome."

Imrial turned toward the boy and seemed ready to ask a question.

"Yes?" he asked her. Her mouth opened but nothing came out. Leo had never seen her so out of her element. "Would you like some advice or information?" All Imrial could do was nod her head. "You have a talent which you know not of - in the near future it will help you in the past."

Leo had to smile. If she was confused before, there was no way this would help. He wasn't surprised though to see her nod her head.

They walked above the floor to the door and into the stairwell. As soon as they stepped out of the room, their feet touched the familiar hard surface of the stairs. The door closed silently behind them.

"Interesting," Leo offered.

"Is that what you call it?" Imrial asked as they headed down the stairs. She had fully regained her voice this time.

"Yes."

She stopped. Her brows were furrowed.

"Don't start with the one-word answers! I'm not in the mood," she said sharply. She had also regained her confidence.

Leo couldn't help smiling.

"So, have you ever seen the Curator?" Leo asked her as she started going down the stairs again.

She hesitated slightly. "No."

"Never? Not even from afar? During a parade, coronation, something?" Leo still hadn't seen anything like a television or, for that matter, a radio.

"No. I hadn't thought about it before, but, I've never seen the Oracles either. Why?"

"Just curious. Who do you think the boy was?" he asked.

They exited on the first floor and made their way out of the building. Imrial had a great sense of direction. Leo was sure she was incapable of getting lost.

"What boy?" she asked.

"The boy in the room with the sand painting on the floor. The boy we just spent the last half-hour playing word games with." They exited into the waning sunlight. Imrial immediately headed off toward the Museum of History.

"There was no boy. We just finished talking to a man

of about thirty years of age, with a long, handlebar mustache."

Leo listened carefully to her voice, and, although she was capable of lying, he didn't believe she was.

"What was the sand painting of?" he asked her.

"It was the Crest of the House of Nahasar. Well done, but nothing spectacular."

"You mean this, right?" Leo showed her the emblem sewn on the inside of the jacket she had gotten for him.

"Yes."

It was nothing like the magnificent thing he had seen.

They walked at a brisk pace.

"I wish we could speak to the Curator," Imrial said.

"Again?" Leo asked, smiling at her.

"Very funny."

Leo never told her he wasn't joking.

Nahasar is credited for being the founding place for many political advances on Elonce. Nahasar was the first of the five nations to introduce the idea of non-hereditary succession. In the year 134 ASC, the throne was occupied by Princess A. M. Tinneb. She was the first of a line of rulers, which ended in 425 ASC. While some successors were related to their predecessors, it is not necessary for this to be the case. King Colton II, changed the level of power the king had when he formed a council of wise men and women to draft a constitution for the nation. Some consider this council a precursor to the Elder Five. Now all nations have forms of checks and balances for their rulers. All rulers have constitutions which dictate the amount of power each actually wields and the form of counter-balances within the governments to ensure no one person has too much power. Political innovation has long been accepted as one of the gifts Nahasar has brought to the five nations.

- H. Cranston, Historian 3rd Class

11

At the Museum of History, there were no guards, just a team of three historians working on a report for the Council on National Historical Preservation.

The three historians moved in slow motion, reviewing a set of floating prisms which emitted a low hum. Each historian wore earphones – or what looked like earphones. Occasionally, one would rotate a floating prism, make notes on a pad, and then go back to whatever it was he was doing. The bottoms of the prisms were a few inches above their chests and were tall enough to reach a few feet above their heads.

Leo looked hard, but couldn't make out any wires holding the prisms up.

He noticed a fourth historian, dressed in the same scholarly garb, pacing on a balcony, looking at a stack of glass covered documents. All the historians were dressed the same, leading him to believe they were all of the same profession, a profession which was obviously entrenched in research. Leo doubted these studious intellectuals ever ventured into the sunlight, except to go to a different museum. Their clothes were unsuited for activity, but well suited for someone needing numerous pockets, cubby-holes, and hide-aways for pads, pencils, and the occasional snack.

The shoes were the same soft, natural material as everyone wore, but the pants looked like leotards covered with layers of flowing robes that reached at the longest to the historians' ankles, and the shortest stopping just below their waists. A mix between an apron and a tool belt was easily visible under the top robe, with straps holding them over each shoulder. These hanging pouches turned out to be extremely useful for holding the more immediate equipment needed in their research. Their hands had a skin colored covering.

Like nylons for their fingers Leo thought.

Imrial, feeling closer to an answer, was not in the mood for demonstrating patience.

"Excuse me, I'm looking for Henders?" she said to the closest Historian. And to ensure that he knew she was speaking to him, she pulled on one of his robes. Firmly.

He turned out to be a she. With the long, 'Scrooge like' nightcaps they all wore, it was impossible to tell male from female unless you saw their faces. And even then, you couldn't be sure.

Leo noticed that the historian looked at Imrial with the confusion of someone disoriented. Looking at her face, he didn't read anger or aggravation for being interrupted in her concentration, just a little surprise. Leo didn't read faces as well as Grans, so he guessed the surprise was because the island was closed and therefore no one should be visiting. Of course, it could have been that she was surprised that anyone would want to see a historian. From what Leo had heard, they were not very highly sought after for conversation.

As if to prove Leo right, she mumbled a quiet "Huh?"

"Henders. I'm looking for a historian named Henders," Imrial tried again, using her command voice.

"Hmm." She looked carefully at her two companions, as if noticing them for the first time.

Imrial turned and looked at Leo with a look between frustration and humor. Humor won out. She gave him a big smile, and then put back on her business face. She turned back to the hapless historian.

Instead of speaking, she pointed at the one Leo had noticed on the balcony. He could have guessed. It's never the one you first speak to, and if there's a group they won't be there either. The one you need is always off by themselves. Leo also knew he would be totally unresponsive. They'd have to beg, plead, or threaten to get any information out of him. It was the way these things always went - at least in every book he'd ever read and every movie he'd ever seen.

The books and movies were all wrong.

They walked up the stairs and Leo approached him first. He thought it would be more correct, since it was his life at risk.

"Excuse me? Henders?" Leo asked.

"Yes? How can I help you?"

"Oh. Well, I'm sorry to disturb you…"

"No worries. I can use a break about now," he said. The historian put a tool into one of his pouches, and then rolled up a scroll he was reading. He put that into his sleeve. He straightened his cap and glasses, and held out his hand.

Leo shook it.

"Henders Cranston, Historian Third-Class. How may I be of service?"

"Leo...Hardy. My friends call me Leo. You can call me Leo." He stumbled over himself quite smoothly. Leo couldn't introduce himself as Leonard Hardy. It would be a lie.

"I know. Everyone knows who you are."

"Oh. Well, I'm trying to find out some information about ...well, there's a rumor." Leo hadn't thought this out in advance.

The historian patiently waited for him to figure out what he wanted to ask.

Imrial wasn't any help. She decided to play protector again and was busy scanning the area for possible threats.

"Someone is supposedly trying to kill me. I wanted to know who was behind it."

Henders nodded his head. He rubbed the seemingly day-old stubble on his chin, and Leo waited.

After a minute that felt like five Henders asked, "Why?"

"Why? Why do I want to know who's trying to kill me?" Leo asked.

"No. That's obvious," he said as he began slowly walking toward a window. "'Why' is the question you should be asking. It's nearly impossible to give a good answer to a bad question."

Leo thought the question, while not worded well, was a good question.

"Who is trying to kill me?" Leo asked. He figured maybe he hadn't understood him the first time.

"I can't tell you that. However, I think what you

should be asking is *why* are they trying to kill you.'"

"If I find out who, I'll be able to figure out why – if that's necessary," Leo argued.

"But if you know why you're at risk, you'll know much more than the who," he countered.

"Ok. Why don't you tell me what you can."

"I'll tell you what I will." He pulled something that looked like a wineskin out of one of his robes. It had a spout like the ones Leo had seen in movies. He popped off the cap and squeezed a smooth stream of blue liquid into his upturned mouth. He offered it to Leo. Leo didn't know if it would be rude to turn him down, so he lifted the skin above his face. Leo only wasted a little on his cheek before he got the stream into his mouth. He wiped his face with his sleeve, getting a smile from Henders in the process. Leo guessed that was not the expected behavior of a king-to-be.

"You really aren't of noble blood, are you?" Henders asked without any meanness.

"No, I'm not," Leo said.

"Well, what do you know of the history of Nahasar? Or the history of Elonce for that matter?"

"Very little, I'm afraid."

"Interesting choice of words. Why are you afraid?"

Then Leo realized what he had said – he knew by now that the innocent sayings he grew up with, could have a much different meaning on Elonce.

"It's just a saying. Like 'luck follows talent.'" Henders didn't seem to believe him, but didn't press it any further.

"Well, the history of the country can tell you a lot. Nahasar's ruler has been picked by the Oracles for the last century."

"Picked? I thought they predicted, not selected a ruler."

"Depends on your viewpoint. Anyway, the Head of the Senate of Nahasar would have normally become the ruler of Nahasar before King Harold. His father was the ruler before Harold, so he was a natural successor. Then the Oracles predicted that Harold would be king. And so he was."

He walked over to the window and opened the vents, letting in the cool, fresh air. He took a deep breath and another swig of liquid. He didn't offer Leo any this time.

"A little disappointed, he joined the Senate. He figured it was for the best, since he was rather young at the time his father stepped down from the throne."

Leo wanted to ask why he had 'stepped down,' but he didn't want to distract the historian. This promised to be the most information anyone had given him, all at one time, since he arrived in this world.

"When King Harold died, Nahasar's constitution called for the Head of the Senate to take over temporarily unless there was a direct descendent. There being no direct descendent, he figured he would finally gain his rightful inheritance – the throne of Nahasar, if only as an interim ruler."

He reached into a pocket and pulled out a small wafer. He chewed it slowly, followed it with another squirt of blue liquid, and swallowed.

"Have you read the Constitution of Nahasar?"

"No, I haven't."

"Hmm" Henders grunted.

Leo didn't like feeling as if he hadn't done his homework. He didn't like feeling like he wasn't qualified for the job. Funny, he never wanted the job, but every time someone acted like he wasn't fit for it, it made him angry.

"Well, there is no provision which would have allowed him to remain king - but once you are crowned, you have a chance of staying in charge. At least, historically it has proven so." Henders seemed to be growing tired of telling the story. He pulled the tool he had been using out of a pocket. With a flourish of his sleeve, the scroll he had been reading appeared.

"As you can tell, it doesn't matter. If the Oracles say differently, it will come to pass. Anyway, when the Oracles picked you so quickly, the Head of the Senate must have felt a bit slighted, as you can imagine."

The historian held out his hand.

Leo looked at his hand, not sure what he wanted. Leo had never paid for anything since he arrived in this world, so he didn't know what to do.

"That's all I have to offer. Good luck," Henders said.

Leo shook his hand, again embarrassed. He was getting seriously tired of feeling like a child. Leo vowed then and there to take charge of his life and stop feeling embarrassed about becoming king.

"Thanks. You've been a great help," he said with a little forcefulness.

"Good." He headed back to his studies.

"Imrial, time to go."

"Imrial, who is the Head of the Senate?" Leo asked as they headed back to the dock.

She had offered to teach him to fly on the way back, but he didn't want to waste any time. He felt energized. He had a direction, a purpose.

"That would be Kanthor J. Noss," she said.

"Do you think he's behind this?" Leo asked. She hadn't participated in the conversation with Henders, but he knew she'd heard every word.

"He could be. I never discount the obvious, but I don't know," she said.

"Noss? Is he related to the windbag?" Leo asked.

"Windbag?" Again, the language thing.

"Is he related to Santore Noss?"

"Yes. He's Santore's uncle." She didn't ask any questions, letting him do his own deducing.

"When we get back, I want an audience with this Kanthor J. Noss." Leo said in his most kingly voice. Instead of the argument he expected, he got a smile from Imrial. Leo guessed it would take a while to change her perception of him, but he could at least put on a good show for everyone else. He was soon to be King of Nahasar.

"Well, you'll see him at dinner tomorrow night with the other leaders of the four countries. He's technically in charge until your coronation, so he's invited to the dinner."

"If he's running the country, why haven't I met with him before?" Leo asked, still trying to sound in-charge.

She smiled even wider. "Because, he's been running the country. Anyway, until your coronation, we didn't think you'd want to be bothered with day-to-day stuff."

"Hmph," he grunted.

"We thought you should spend your time learning the language and staying alive."

Leo knew she was right, and he hadn't shown any interest in the other stuff until now. He was busy trying to fit in, and to convince himself that this whole thing wasn't a long, silly dream.

"Well, I'd still like to speak to him alone."

"Alone?"

"If I'm going to be the King of Nahasar, I guess it's time I started acting like it," he said.

"By putting yourself in danger? This trip was bad enough, now you want to be alone with the man who could be trying to kill you? Does acting like a king mean being foolish?"

Now Leo had to smile. "You can be there, if you like."

"Now you're starting to sound like a king," she said.

"How's that?"

"Wise, very wise."

They laughed most of the way back to the ship.

When they reached the dock there was a flyer landing. They watched the pilot make a perfect landing on the smooth water. A side door opened and a ramp soundlessly extended to the dock. One of the Elders stepped out, and walked across. The guard bowed.

The Elder (Leo still had trouble telling them apart) said something they couldn't hear and then headed toward them. He came straight up to them, and addressed Imrial.

"Miss Imrial, it's time you and the young king-to-be headed back." His blue robes seemed new. He bowed to Leo and then straightened, waiting for them to leave. Something about his demeanor made Leo think he hadn't come for them.

"Are you coming?" Leo asked.

"No, I have business here," he said.

"Oh," was all Leo could think to say at first. They took a step toward their craft, and Leo turned back to him again.

"Elder, you wouldn't be planning to see the Oracles, would you?" Leo wasn't sure how he knew – it could have been more of a wish than a guess.

"Yes, I am. I have to escort them to your coronation tomorrow, and there are a few details we have to discuss." That was the most information an elder had ever offered, without him prodding. Except for Henders Cranston, everyone seemed tight-lipped. Leo looked at the elder, patiently. There was more, otherwise he wouldn't have told him so much.

"Hmm," Leo said, waiting.

"Sire, you really must get back," the Elder said. Not what Leo expected or wanted to hear.

"Yes, but…" Leo let it hang there between them. He thought the Elder would offer more if he waited him out, if for no other reason than to end the conversation. He seemed to be in a rush and Leo thought he wouldn't want to waste more time than necessary speaking with him.

Leo was wrong. Again.

The Elder just stood there waiting. Very attentive. Very polite. Very respectful. And very infuriating!

Leo finally gave in.

"Is it possible for me to speak with the oracles?" He asked, already knowing the answer.

"No, I'm sorry, Sire. It is forbidden for anyone to have a private audience with the oracles," he said and waited again.

Another five minutes went by before Leo once again gave in. Perhaps the elder wasn't in as much of a rush as Leo had thought.

"But it wouldn't be a private…"

"I'm sorry. I meant that it is not permissible for anyone, other than the Elder Five or the Curator, to see them, except in a public setting."

"Well…" Leo began to try an argument.

"'Public,' meaning at a fully public event. Like your coronation. You'll see them then."

Leo waited for another thirty seconds before he gave up. He knew he was going to give up, but he waited anyway, out of spite. He wasn't proud of it, but he was angry. He didn't want to accept their silly rules. Anyway, the elder didn't seem to mind. Once Leo and Imrial took off, they could see him waving before turning and heading off to the Oracles' secret "bat cave."

"So, I'll make a deal with you," Imrial began. They were flying back toward the castle, and the sun was starting to set.

"Do kings make deals with security agents?" He asked. He didn't mean it as an insult, but she took it as one.

"I'm not some three-horse tracker, working the..." she was growling the words at him. Leo didn't need to use his talents to tell he had pushed a button.

"Sorry. I didn't mean anything." He cut off her lecture. "Didn't you see my smile?" She hadn't been looking at him of course, she was busy flying. Leo made sure she could hear the smile in his voice this time.

It worked, and she smiled herself.

"No, I'm sorry," she said.

"So, what exactly *are* you? I saw how the guards at the island treated you, and the servants back at the castle, and even the elders. You're not *just* an agent, are you?"

"Wrong question," she said, and he could see her smile broaden. She was teasing him, mimicking Henders Cranston.

"Oh really?" he asked.

"You should have asked, '*who* exactly are you.'"

"Well?" Leo asked.

"Let's see. I was going to offer to take you to see the city. With the sun setting, it will be one of the most beautiful sights you've ever seen."

"And what must I do in exchange?" he asked, ignoring her evasion of his question.

"Hold off meeting with Kanthor J. Noss until tomorrow night." She glanced over at him, and then back to the control panel. She made a slight adjustment of a dial and then went back to watching the horizon. It was an easy deal to make. Leo really wasn't losing anything. He could deduce that if Kanthor J. Noss was running the country, he would not be able to drop everything to meet with him tonight anyway. The best Leo would get is to see him tomorrow, so he wasn't really giving up anything.

"Sure," he said, "and later we can make another deal."

"Really?"

"Yes, I'd like to know what..." he corrected himself, "...who you really are."

"Oh? And what do you have to offer?" she asked.

"The same thing I want from you - information." That was the same on Elonce as on Earth. Information was power, and a valuable commodity.

"We'll barter in a moment," she said as she banked the craft to the right. She dipped the craft down, and they swooped toward the ground. About fifty feet off the surface she leveled them out. The city loomed ahead of them; the beautiful metal gleam they had seen on the way to the Island of Museums was bathed in deep reds, oranges, and edged with dark purples and blues. It was truly magnificent. Flying ships, with running lights on, moving in and out between the buildings, looked like fire-flies darting about. When the buildings started to block the sunset, she pulled back on the controls and they rose on a steep incline. She kept climbing until Leo thought they were going to leave the atmosphere (judging distances definitely was not one of his talents). With little effort, she made five quick adjustments and the craft stalled, dipped forward and seemed to hover in place. She extended both sets of wings (one normally used for low flight, and the other for landings) and cut the engines. Leo didn't think the engines made any noise, but he was wrong. They had a soft, murmuring hum which was now noticeable by its absence. She opened the front air vents, and they could hear the wind blowing around them.

They were gliding. She played with the rudder controls and they dipped, swayed, and floated in a perfect sweeping arc toward the city below. The sounds of the wind, the view, and the smooth flight of the craft all combined to create one of the most beautiful experiences of Leo's life. He glanced over at Imrial and realized she was working feverishly to make this possible. She kept adjusting dials, playing the control pedals with her feet, and pulling and pushing this lever or that. The craft wasn't made for gliding. He knew he had gotten the better end of the deal. Leo went back to enjoying the view.

Leo made his second deal with Imrial right after they landed. She was shutting down the engines and performing a post-flight check.

"So, who exactly are you?" Leo asked.

"No one special, really. But my parents have a little pull in political circles. They're the King and Queen of Terrence." She told him this very nonchalantly and he realized she was being honest. Not just about being a princess, but about not feeling it was anything special.

It was not what he expected.

"So, now you know 'who' I am," she said smiling, "so what's your information?"

"Are you sure you've been honest with me? It's not exactly one of your talents," Leo said smiling. He wanted to make her wait for his information.

"Yes. Unless the oracles predicted that I was to be the queen of something, I'm allowed to become anything I want."

"And your parents were ok with you becoming an agent?" he asked. Even if it were allowed, he doubted that a king and queen would want their daughter to be a military agent.

"I didn't say that."

"No, you didn't," Leo agreed, remembering how headstrong she could be, "but I thought you were from Nahasar?"

"I am. You don't have to be from the same country to marry the king. Didn't that ever happen on Earth?" she asked.

"Yes, actually, it did," he said, remembering a few times that he knew of. "Which nation are you the princess of?"

"Well, I don't think of myself as a 'princess'."

"But that's what you are. I mean your parents are the king and queen of…"

"Terence."

"…Terence. So, you're the princess of Terence, right?"

"Yes, I guess technically I'm a princess. I just don't make a big deal of it. Remember, we don't pick kings and queens by birth," she reminded him.

"I thought that was only in Nahasar?" Leo asked.

"Nope. Nahasar was the first to stop hereditary succession, but all the nations have adopted it."

"That's right. The oracles pick your rulers," he added.

She pulled a lever and the doors opened. The ramp was already extended out and down to the ground.

"Enough stalling, what's this information I'll be so happy about?" she asked as she started unbuckling her harness.

"Oh, just that I know who the assassin in the castle is," he said as he walked out of the craft. He looked around and saw Young Philip. The giant was sitting in a kind of rocking chair, reading a book. When he saw Leo coming toward him, he put the book down and rose from the chair. When they were a few feet apart, Young Philip bowed.

"Sire," he said as he finished his bow. Leo smiled at

his bow and the use of 'sire.' Leo wanted to tease him about it, but he didn't seem the type to take it well.

"Did you check on Sean?" Leo asked as Imrial came up behind him.

"You know *what*?" she whispered hard in his ear. It was so loud a whisper, there was no way Young Philip didn't hear it.

"Yes, he is doing much better," Young Philip said.

Leo turned to Imrial. "I said I know who the assassin is. The one you've been looking for."

"Who? How?"

"Young Philip can take you to him," Leo said as he headed back to his rooms. Leo wanted to turn and see her face so badly, but didn't. He knew her mouth was hanging open in shock.

"Why didn't you say something before we left?" she yelled after him.

"Would you have taken me to the island if I had?" He yelled back, without turning. Leo needed to speak with Grans. There was a lot of planning to do before he confronted Kanthor J. Noss.

Etiquette is not only a preferred skill for young men and women seeking higher status, it is a necessity. Through etiquette we learn to interact with our superiors and thereby raise ourselves to the desired position of peer. Etiquette is the essence of culture.

> - Jean Philippe Theiro, trainer of
>   princes, princesses, and aspirants

Forget "etiquette", just pass the gravy!

> - Prince Kairo on the eve of Jean
>   Philippe Theiro's resignation

12

The dinner was a grand affair.

The delegates from the other four nations of Elonce arrived within fifteen minutes of each other. Unlike on Earth, the powerful of Elonce arrived early, rather than fashionably late. Each had a small entourage, which seemed more like a group of hairdressers and servants than security guards, although Imrial assured Leo they were both.

The King of Terence was the first to arrive, accompanied by his wife. They wore sparkling, highly-formal gowns. The King seemed nice enough, although a little stand-offish. He may have been wondering why Leo was studying them so hard - he was trying to see which of them Imrial took after. She had her mother's hair, a beautiful fiery red beneath a small tiara. She had her father's eyes and forceful chin. Leo shook their hands, holding them a little longer than normal.

Next came the President of Europa with his two daughters and a nephew. Imrial whispered that the nephew was forced upon the president, for the opportunity to meet with the leaders of Elonce. She said the rumor was that the President had to pay a debt to his sister. Leo asked her if, once he became king, there would be as many rumors about him. She said there were already more rumors about him than any other leader, ever.

Next was the Vice President of Afrisia, the largest of the continents. She apologized for the absence of the President, explaining that he was ill.

Next came Kanthor J. Noss, the Head of the Senate of Nahasar. Leo watched him very closely. He came alone, and dressed in royal colors – acting like the ruler of Nahasar instead of the stand-in for the crown. Leo took an immediate dislike to him. Of course, suspecting he was behind the assassination attempts didn't help.

The next guest was a representative for the Curator. A nice young man, a little older than Leo. Leo liked him immediately. He seemed as uncomfortable in this crowd as Leo was. The young man fiddled with his clothes constantly, pulling and tugging here and there.

Then came the co-rulers of Amedia. They were gloriously dressed, their clothes giving off light. Not just reflecting light, but actually illuminating the space around them. It gave them a very unique look. Leo couldn't help thinking of how useful they'd be if there was a blackout.

The last to arrive were the Elder Five. Grans told Leo at least one would be attending, but they all showed up, together. They were obviously agitated. Something had happened, but Leo didn't get a chance to ask about it before the formal ceremonies began.

Grans was on Leo's right and Santore Noss on his left. Imrial sat behind and to his left as his personal bodyguard. Leo didn't like having a bodyguard, but he was happy to have her sitting nearby. Leo had argued with Grans and Imrial that he wanted Imrial sitting at the table, but they won out in the end – reminding him that he may need all the support he could get from the attendees, and choosing the seating arrangement was not a battle worth fighting.

Leo found the food to be excellent, familiar, and just a little...off. It was like having frozen yogurt instead of ice cream. It was good, very good. It tasted something like what it should, but not exactly. There were meats, vegetables, breads, fruits, lots of drinks, and they all were very good. But wrong. They almost tasted like foods on Earth, but not quite. This was another thing he'd have to investigate if he had time. There seemed to be a lot of things that were similar to life back on Earth, but Leo needed more time to research it. Time he didn't have.

What Leo did have time for was starting a little trouble.

Immediately after the last plate was cleared, the glasses were filled with wine for the final toast.

He stood up, with full glass in hand. He looked around the table, purposefully establishing eye contact with each one in turn (as Grans had recommended). Then he offered a toast. It would be the talk of Nahasar, if not all of Elonce, for days to come.

"To the reign of Leonard Hardy's blood-line as rulers of Nahasar, to the memory of my grandfather the late, the great, Leonard Hardy."

A cheer of "hear, hear" went up before anyone realized what it meant.

Then most turned to the person next to them to ask, "Was his grandfather named Leonard, too?" And before they could debate the question, Kanthor J. Noss stood up to clarify the issue.

"You are not Leonard Hardy! You are an impostor!" Kanthor bellowed, as if announcing a proclamation.

Silence filled the hall.

"Yes and no." Leo answered very calmly. Leo's gaze was fully locked on Kanthor. "Yes, I am not Leonard Hardy, I am his grandson." For effect, he downed his glass. "And no, I am not an impostor…I am the rightful heir of the throne of Nahasar, as proclaimed by the Oracles."

Although many argued that it was not rehearsed, both Grans and Imrial had coached him for hours on how to say this just right. Grans beamed with pride at how well it came off, and how un-practiced it sounded.

"By your own admission, you are an impostor!" Kanthor J. Noss slammed his glass down, spilling wine on the table cloth.

"I am the rightful heir of the throne of Nahasar, as proclaimed by the Oracles." Leo repeated, still staring at his adversary. Still calm. "Read the record of the proclamation!"

Santore Noss rose on cue, pulled a scroll from his robe and cleared his throat. He glanced only once at Kanthor J. Noss, and then pressed on importantly.

"The Oracles, on the day of the death of King Harold of Nahasar, announced." Here he paused. "The blood-line of Leonard Hardy will rule for the next five generations." He rolled the scroll back up, latched it closed and added, "And a DNA sample was provided for proof of identity."

"Then I demand to see the proof that you are of Leonard Hardy's blood!" Kanthor yelled.

"An assassin chased me across time to kill me because he knew I would fulfill the prophecy. He spent his life finding a way back to Elonce and when he returned he injured a guard, and would have killed anyone in his way." Leo put his glass down slowly.

"If I remember the accounts correctly, the assassin, as

you call him, was sent back to retrieve the true future King of Nahasar – Leonard Hardy. And, when he found out that you, an impostor, had come back, did everything in his power to stop you."

"Do you deny that he was an assassin?"

Kanthor ignored the question.

"Do you deny that he called you an impostor when he attacked? There is no proof that he was trying to kill you, or that he was an assassin. But there may be proof that you are an impostor!"

"Enough!" Grans stood up.

"Who are you? What say do you have in this?" Kanthor asked the question most of the guests had on their minds. Ever since Leo's return with Imrial and Grans, rumors ran rampant over who the older woman was.

"I am the counselor chosen by the future King." Answering while avoiding answering the question. "I will give you the proof you seek." Grans waved for the nurse standing by the door. The nurse hurried over to the table and held out a small round tube to Leo. He breathed into the tube and handed it back. The nurse put the tube into a metal ring. She then pulled out a second ring. It held a DNA sample of Leonard Hardy. After a few moments, she removed the ring from the tube and put both rings on the table. Everyone watched, excited that the normal, boring political dinner had become quite a fun hullabaloo.

The rings hummed slightly, as DNA signatures rose above them in holographic projections.

Leo tore his eyes away from Kanthor to see the effect. It was like something out of a science fiction movie. The DNA strands, made up of all the colors of the rainbow, slowly rotated above the rings. One of them stopped turning. The second one turned, stopped, turned in the opposite direction and then stopped again. The nurse held out a small device like a handheld computer. She pressed two buttons and reexamined the projections, made a note on the device, and announced…

"Leonard…I mean Leo Hardy is of the same DNA as Leonard Hardy."

"But…" Kanthor J. Noss began.

"I'm not through," the nurse shot a glare at him.

He glowered back.

"And, the data affirms that Leo Hardy is the grandson of Leonard Hardy." She smiled at Leo, and then nodded to Kanthor.

"But…" Kanthor said in a lower volume. He had lost most of his energy.

"I offer two more proofs, as required by custom," Grans said. "Elder Five, you have examined Leo Hardy?"

The Fifth Elder, again in white, looking more lively than normal, stood up.

"Yes, I have. He has seven talents, like his grandfather. We are satisfied that he is who he says he is." Leo looked over at the Elder Five. The Fifth was standing, doing his part, while the other four remained seated. He so wanted to ask them what his other talents were, but again his personal needs and curiosity had to wait.

Kanthor J. Noss pointed at Grans, "but, how can you know all this? How do you know our customs? You're not even of this world!" He had regained some of his confidence and redirected his anger at Grans.

It was time for all truths to be known.

"I swore my allegiance to Nahasar years ago, in truth, a lifetime ago. I am Genevieve De Scioncia Hardy, agent of the Nahasar Nation, wife of the late Leonard Hardy, grandmother of Leo Hardy, the rightful heir of

Nahasar." As if on cue, the nurse approached the table again. She handed Grans a tube. She took it from her and breathed into it. The nurse took the tube and placed the other end into a metal ring.

"I offer the third proof – an eyewitness account. I was present and aware, when the son of Leonard Hardy, Leon Hardy, my son was born. I attest that he was our son. I was also present and aware when Leo Hardy, my grandson, was born, and I attest that he is the grandson of Leonard Hardy, the same Leonard Hardy the Oracles proclaimed as the father of the line of rulers of Nahasar for the next five generations!"

Kanthor's mouth dropped open. He sat down in his chair, shaking his head.

Leo also sat down, once again focused, only on Kanthor.

The Nurse pulled the ring off the tube and placed it on the table. A third holograph was projected. After a moment, the nurse proclaimed...

"This is Genevieve De Scioncia, and she is the grandmother of Leo Hardy."

Applause broke out around the table. Cheers could be heard in the kitchen and the hallways outside the room. Grans sat down, satisfied with her declaration.

Imrial slipped quietly from her chair, and moved behind Kanthor J. Noss.

When the clapping finally died down, Kanthor found his voice. He was obviously shaken by the completeness of the declaration. Any hopes he had of proving Leo an impostor were gone. He stood up, clearing his throat.

"I recant my accusation, and beg your pardon. You are the rightful heir of Nahasar and I look forward to passing on the power of the Nation to you tomorrow night." Leo was impressed. He made his statement with more strength than Leo had anticipated, although he was obviously defeated.

"Does this mean the attempts on my life will cease?" Leo asked. He didn't feel like he had won anything. He always knew who he was. His enemy just made it easier for him to prove himself. Now, Leo was ready for the real fight. Kanthor seemed ill-prepared for the attack.

"I...I don't understand," Kanthor J. Noss said. He looked around the table, but every face he met was an accusatory one.

"The assassin you defended a moment before, murdered my grandfather, Leonard Hardy."

"I didn't, I didn't know," he kept shaking his head.

"And you have the most to gain from my death...you would remain in charge, a position you believe is rightfully yours. Do you deny it?" Leo was back on his feet. When he rose, Imrial motioned to two guards and approached Kanthor from behind.

"No, no. That would be true. But..." At this Imrial grabbed his chair and the two guards lifted him from the seat by his arms.

"You're under arrest," Imrial said as she dramatically threw the chair backward.

"No!"

"Yes," Imrial calmly corrected him, "and we have further proof of your guilt."

Imrial had everyone's attention.

"We caught another assassin in the palace, yesterday evening. He was an assistant mechanic brought into the palace just recently," Imrial started, as the guards began ushering Kanthor J. Noss toward the door.

"He was from your household," Imrial continued.

"But, who..." Kanthor tried.

"Sean Bulthoware. He also said that his orders came from you," Imrial finished.

The guards exited with Noss between them. After a

few moments, the commotion died down. Leo was still standing, leaning on his hands. He was exhausted from the confrontation.

"Sire, you'll need to name a new Head of the Senate." The First Elder stood as he spoke.

"But Kanthor J. has not been found guilty, yet," added the Second Elder, standing.

"True, but he cannot rule over his own trial, and neither can the accuser," said the Fourth, rising in turn.

"I know. Thank you." Leo sat down, and the Elders followed his lead and sat also.

"Who will you name to lead the senate?" asked the King of Terence.

"Until the coronation, and until the Senate can reconvene, I appoint Genevieve De Scioncia Hardy as Head of the Senate." The proclamation was followed by many 'oohs' and 'aahs,' but no argument.

"Wise choice," said the Fifth Elder.

"A very wise choice," the Third agreed.

Throughout history, wisdom is referred to as a woman. Even Solomon, the most famous wise man in biblical history anointed wisdom with a feminine gender. Solomon stated that wisdom would never enter a soul living in deceit. Deception and wisdom cannot coexist. Internal and external forms of deceit kill the seed of wisdom.

- Fr. Jose Martinez, unpublished manuscript, 1987

13

The morning of the coronation should have been a glorious dawn. The man behind the assassination plot was in chains awaiting his hearing, an assassin was captured before he could do any harm, and the coronation was soon to go as planned. The morning should have been bright with promise.

But, it wasn't.

It was a bleak, wet, morning. A fog covered the area, misting the palace grounds. Leo was in a bad mood, Imrial was barking angrily at anyone foolish enough to approach her, and even Genevieve was tired from a poor night's sleep.

All of this should have boded poorly for Kanthor J. Noss, but Genevieve wasn't one for omens. She believed truth always won out in the end, and she wasn't sure the truth was obvious in this case.

Before breakfast, Genevieve De Scioncia called for the hearing of Kanthor J. Noss.

The prisoner was brought before her in the throne room. One guard stood on either side of him, fully focused on their prisoner. Kanthor held his head low in shame and dejection. His life was over.

The actual throne wasn't in the room, as it was getting a last minute polishing for the ceremony, so Genevieve sat on a small stool on the dais where the throne normally was. Kanthor J. Noss had to stand, in chains. Imrial stood to the right of the dais with two more guards.

Genevieve followed the traditional process. "You know the allegations against you. You know the evidence. What have you to say?"

Kanthor also followed accepted procedure, albeit with no enthusiasm. "I am innocent of all charges."

"Why should I believe you in the face of evidence that says otherwise?" This was not normal. Genevieve was supposed to ask him if he wanted counsel, and if so, who. Then a date was to be set for a trial. This caught everyone off guard, especially Noss.

"I don't understand…I…"

"Do you believe in the Oracles' power of prediction?" Genevieve helped.

"Of course. They were given the power by the Curator, and they've never been wrong."

"Can they be?" Genevieve asked.

"No, they aren't making guesses, they actually see the future," he answered sullenly. His head still hung with his chin almost resting on his chest.

"You mean to tell me that the Oracles are infallible? They can't make a mistake?" she prodded.

"No, they can't. At least, not in their predictions."

"So, can Leo Hardy be assassinated before he has an heir?" Genevieve asked.

"No."

"Look at me," she said with stern compassion. He raised his head.

Genevieve studied Kanthor's face carefully. She had already checked with the Elder Five and confirmed her suspicion that he did not have the talent of deception. She knew she'd be able to tell his heart by looking at his face.

"Why would you plot to kill Leo Hardy if you knew it was impossible to succeed?"

Kanthor finally caught on. His face brightened and a smile actually creased his lips. He straightened up and looked Genevieve in the eyes for the first time since entering the room. Tears formed in his eyes.

"I wouldn't. I fully believe in the power of the Oracles and any attempt to kill Leo Hardy would be a foolhardy one." He got on a roll. "And to attempt to kill him, without hoping to succeed would even be more idiotic."

"And, Kanthor J. Noss, Head of the Senate of Nahasar, are you, or were you ever, a fool?"

"No, ma'am, I am not." The chains were the only thing keeping Kanthor from grabbing Genevieve's hands and showering them with kisses.

Imrial took a step forward. She realized what Genevieve was doing, and wasn't sure how to react.

"Then I find you innocent of all charges and reinstate you to the position to which you rightfully belong. Remove his chains." She stood up and walked toward Kanthor.

The guards, like Imrial, weren't sure what to do. They looked at each other and then to Imrial. Imrial only hesitated a moment. It didn't matter if she fully understood - she knew her job. She nodded to the guards.

The guards removed Kanthor's chains and took a step back.

Kanthor, normally very prim and proper, ignored ceremony and met Genevieve before she reached the last step. He bowed deeply, almost brushing his face on the floor. Genevieve bowed back.

"Thank you, my lady."

"You're very welcome. Now, I must tell my grandson that his enemy has yet to be found."

Imrial had fully believed that Kanthor was their man. Now, she was totally confused. She caught up to Genevieve as she was leaving the room.

"Jenny," she called softly.

"Yes, Immy?"

"What about the testimony of the boy? The one sent to kill Leo?"

"Nonsense. He said that he was told Noss was behind it, but never met him. He only received his orders from a messenger. A messenger that also told him that if he didn't kill Leo, his family would be killed."

"Not exactly a good source for the truth," Imrial agreed.

"No, he told the truth as he knew it."

"So, who *is* behind it all?" Imrial asked.

"I don't know. But I think there's one person with the talent to deduce the answer."

Talent - 1. A natural ability to do a task well. 2. An unnatural ability to do a task exceptionally well. 3. A hereditary trait manifested through the uncanny ability to do something beyond the explainable.

- Dictionary of traits, 1st Printing, House of Terrence

Talent - An exceptionally high level of skill demonstrated without the corresponding transfer of knowledge.

- Conclusion from doctoral dissertation, The Fourth Elder, School of Thought.

14

Leo had a lousy night and felt uneasy all morning. He couldn't sleep for more than an hour at a time before waking from bad dreams. Leo couldn't remember any of them, but he knew they weren't pleasant. It was as if something were trying to warn him of some danger.

When Imrial and Grans told him that Kanthor was freed, he was even more upset.

Genevieve explained three times how she had read Kanthor's face during dinner and knew he was innocent. Leo finally had to listen, although he was still unhappy about it. It was something he thought was over, done, completed. He had mentally checked that off of his "to do" list. Found person behind the assassination attempts on my life, *check*.

He knew Grans was right, or at least he trusted her talents.

Genevieve told him how she was up all night also, but not due to bad dreams. She didn't know how to prove

Kanthor's innocence, but she knew she had to. Otherwise the real criminal would have a free hand to plan an attack.

"We'll find the person behind all of this, don't worry," Imrial said, obviously trying to make him feel better.

"That's not it, or not all of it," Leo said. Grans just stared at him thoughtfully. "There's something else bothering me…I just don't know what."

"Too bad you had to let Kanthor go…" Imrial started.

"I couldn't let him…" Genevieve began.

"I know. No, I mean let him go in public. It could have benefited us to have the real enemy think we had the wrong man and he…"

"Or she," Leo added.

"Or she, might become sloppy or overconfident. Now our enemy will continue to be careful." Imrial finished. They sat quietly, each trying to think of a plan, or their next step.

"Well, we can go back to the Curator…maybe they'll let us see him this time instead of some lackey," Imrial said.

"Grans, would the Curator lie?"

Genevieve had been very quiet. Now she looked at Leo with surprise. No, it was shock on her face.

"No, I didn't think so," Leo concluded.

"What are you talking about?" Imrial asked. "We didn't even talk to the Curator!"

Leo didn't help her, though he felt a little guilty not cluing her in.

"So, if the Curator was accurate, and Henders had the answers I sought…" Leo thought out loud.

Imrial started to pout.

"Henders chose not to share those answers. Instead he led me down a false trail" Leo said.

Grans kept quiet a little while longer.

"Guard!" Leo yelled.

The guard outside the door came in quickly.

"Yes, Sire?"

"Where can I find an Elder?"

"Which one, Sire?"

"Any will do," he said.

"Would you like me to get one for...?"

"No, no. Just tell me where I can find him."

"Follow me, Sire." Leo got another smile from a security guard. It seemed he had an eighth talent - humoring the help.

Leo followed the guard, Grans followed, still quiet, and Imrial followed Grans, shaking her head.

They went up two flights of stairs and down a long corridor, to a closed, ornate door.

Leo knocked.

"One moment, please."

When the Elder came to the door, Leo was a little disappointed to see it was the Second Elder. He had been secretly hoping for the Fifth Elder, but, as it turned out, what you need isn't always what you want.

"Sorry to bother you, but I need some information," Leo said, as the Elder beckoned them into the small room.

"I am at your service," he said. The room was a guest room, and not a very spectacular one. It was a simple room. More of what Leo expected for a monk then for a representative of the Curator and an Elder. Leo's surprise at the room must have shown on his face – part of that honesty talent – because the Elder immediately explained.

"I asked for this room. I think better with no distractions. I find too much decoration and luxury to be *very* distracting."

"I understand," Leo said.

He waved the three of them to a small sitting couch. Grans and Leo sat down. The Elder sat in a modest rocker-type chair across from them. Imrial stationed the guard outside the room and closed the door. Leo nodded to her, but she wasn't looking at him. She was scanning the room as normal. She'd stand by the door the whole time, ready for anything.

"I have a question about one of the historians. Henders Cranston, do you know him?"

"Yes, I do. He happens to be from Terence, my home."

"What is his background? How did he become a historian?" Leo was pretty sure of his reasoning, but he wanted confirmation this time. He wanted to be absolutely sure.

"He became a historian about twenty years ago. As a second career."

"Do you know why?"

"His original career path was no longer possible, at least if you believe in the Oracles," he said. Leo had grown used to the story-telling way everyone on Elonce spoke. Although he didn't feel like it, he would have to be patient.

"Back when Henders was a child, he was groomed to be the King of Terence. His father loved him very much, and was looking forward to the day he could crown Henders as King. 'William the Good' was what people called his father. His wife, Henders' mother, died during Henders' childbirth, so William, King of Terence, raised Henders with all the love he had. He never remarried, never had any other children." The Elder paused to sip a cup of tea.

"Henders grew up always knowing his future, knowing he'd be king. He even knew when - on his seventeenth birthday. Unlike most heirs, who wait for the day their father (or mother) dies or becomes incapable of ruling, Henders *knew* the day he'd be king." The Elder put the cup down and leaned back in the chair. It looked to be quite a comfortable chair.

"William wanted his son to have everything. He wanted his son to be happy. And famous. He didn't want anything for himself, which is why he was a very good king." He let this last statement hang in the air for a while.

Leo nodded, letting him know he got the message.

"Unfortunately, William wasn't very bright. He wanted so much for his son, but he never told anyone his plans. Henders was groomed from birth to be king, but in his seventeenth year of life, the preparations became accelerated. He spent every waking moment of that year learning to be king. On the eve of his birthday, he had a final visit from his loving father."

"Final visit?" Leo asked. He actually forgot that he was trying to find who was behind his assassination.

"Yes," the Elder paused again. "William the Good had decided to turn over the crown on his son's birthday. The laws of Terence allow for a king to give up the crown before death, but only if the king goes into exile. That way, there is no chance that he will change his mind and create a problem."

Grans shook her head in sadness.

"So, that night, William the Good told his son, his only son, his beloved son, that he would be king in the morning. That he would be crowned King of Terence and that he should rule with kindness, mercy, and love. Then he disappeared."

Leo wanted to ask questions, but restrained himself, and waited.

"The next morning, Henders woke up, believing he'd

be king." The Elder paused for effect, looked carefully at Leo and Genevieve, and then continued.

"His father had left a note, stating that he was going into exile voluntarily, giving the throne over to his son. The note was found by a maid and given over to the Lead Councilor, who immediately contacted us. We authenticated the note and, as always when a ruler of one of the five nations is lost to us, we consulted the Oracles."

"What was the normal procedure in Terence?" Leo knew the interruption would be unwelcome, but he couldn't stop his mouth.

The Elder looked disappointed. He took another sip from his cup, coughed, and then returned to the story as if Leo hadn't spoken.

"The Oracles, as always, already knew, and were ready for us. They proclaimed the next king would be Jonathan Shearcoat, a nobleman of Terence. He was crowned the King of Terence three nights later." The Elder looked at Leo, seeing if he'd ask another question. When no questions were offered, he continued.

"Young Henders was upset, but he was also very smart. Unlike his father, he decided to consult the Oracles before making any hasty decisions. Through the Elder Five, he asked three pointed questions. How long would Jonathan be king, who would be the next king, and would he, Henders, ever be king." He put down his cup and sat back. The story was almost over.

"Since the Oracles can only predict the next ruler (if near the time of succession) and events of large magnitude, they could not answer his questions. "

Leo looked at him with disbelief.

"The fact that Leonard Hardy's line would rule for five generations *is* a large scale event," he answered Leo's silent question, only slightly irritated.

"When the Oracles couldn't answer his questions, he flew into a rage. His father was gone, he had no family left, and now he had no future. He turned to his only friend, or at least who he considered a friend. The Lead Councilor for Terence. The Lead Councilor advised him to study the rules and history of Terence if he wanted to someday be king. To help with this, he got him a job as a historian-in-training."

Leo nodded in understanding. "He has spent twenty years studying the history and rules of his country, and decided he would never be king," Leo added.

The Second Elder sat watching him think it through. It was all guesswork, part of the story, which hadn't been written yet.

"Unless…" Leo said, thinking aloud, working it out, "…unless the Oracles were wrong in the first place. If he could prove the Oracles were capable of error, then he could claim the throne." Leo stood up and began to pace the small room.

"He would have to prove one of their predictions to be false…one that had not come true yet. Like a five generation rule, when there is only one left in the line. If I am killed or have no heirs, the Oracles would be wrong." Leo was on a roll.

"He would have a lifetime to kill me. It wouldn't have to be before the coronation. As long as the Oracles are proven wrong," Leo said.

"Hmm. We hadn't thought of that" the Elder admitted.

"So you knew all along that it was Henders?" Leo asked

"No. I meant we hadn't considered that your life would still be in danger after the coronation."

"Well?"

"Very interesting," the Second Elder said.

"But…" Leo stopped pacing and faced the Second Elder. "…if he succeeds, it's not only the rulership of Terence which would be up for grabs, so would every country's top position, since the Oracles select…" he got a stern look from the Elder, "…predict…" and now a smile, "…each successor."

"Why do the Oracles only predict rulers and large events?" Leo asked.

"That is an excellent question, young sire," he said approvingly.

"Great, cause I'm hoping for an excellent answer," Leo replied, happy with his deductions.

"That is the only power the Curator gave them."

"Why? Why not give them the power to tell the whole future?"

"The Curator used to do that himself. He'd answer any and every question asked of him. But he soon realized that people became lazy. They stopped trying, stopped growing. There was no surprise left, no wonder, no learning. They stopped thinking. So he stopped answering questions."

"And?" Leo was too wound up to be patient any longer.

"And he found that, without any guidance, our worst side came out. We had many wars, crimes, and catastrophes. Some brought on by ourselves, some by nature. In either case, we were unprepared to deal with them and many died or suffered. So he tried a third way – the Oracles." The Second Elder picked up his cup again.

Leo had enough to go on…

"So, he gave the Oracles the power to predict successors so there would be no fighting over rulership." He started pacing again. "And, the power to predict large events, so we could be prepared for them or avoid them altogether," Leo said, not realizing his use of 'we.'

"If the Oracles predicted the outcome of wars, there would be no need to fight them." He stopped pacing. "So, if he succeeds in killing me, there will be a lot more trouble than just who rules Terence."

"Very, very interesting," the Elder decided.

"Thank you," Leo said as he headed toward the door.

"So you don't believe?" the Second Elder started to rock again.

"Don't believe what?" Leo knew he wouldn't answer. He had to figure it out. But instead, all he could think about was how easily Henders had sent him down the wrong path and the signs he had missed. Henders had used a lot of half-truths but Leo should have been able to figure it out. Finally what the Elder was getting at struck him.

"You mean you don't believe he *can* kill me. You mean I can't die?"

"That's not totally accurate," he said.

"You mean the Oracles can't be wrong, and somehow the Leonard Hardy line *will* rule for five generations."

"Congratulations," the Elder said. Four days ago Leo would have thought his comment odd. Now he took it as a compliment and an affirmation.

"But even if I believe, Henders can still cause a lot of pain and hurt a lot of people."

The Second Elder nodded.

Leo turned to go and noticed that Imrial was gone. He looked at Grans, but the surprised look on her face told him that she didn't know when Imrial had left the room either nor where she had gotten off to.

"Imrial!" Leo shouted as he opened the door. The guard was still stationed outside the room.

"Sire, she left about ten minutes ago."

"No!" Leo turned to Grans.

"Go. And hurry," she said.

Leo turned back to the guard, "I need to get to the Museum of History, like yesterday!"

"Sire?" He looked at Leo, confused, and then Leo remembered that he was known as the Time Warp King for a reason beyond his appearance in the country.

"It's a figure of speech, it means I need to get there as fast as possible."

"Yes, Sire!" He led the way to the garage, running the whole way. The other guard followed. It seemed that he was going to have two escorts anywhere he went. He knew without asking that Imrial had left orders to that effect before she slipped away.

When Leo reached the garage, young Philip informed him that she did indeed have a ten-minute head start on him. It took another fifteen minutes to round up a pilot. When they finally started, they were thirty minutes behind Imrial. The pilot got on the communications system and called ahead. When he reached the Captain of the Guard for the Island of Museums he gave the device to Leo.

"This is Leo Hardy…"

"Yes, Sire?" The woman's voice was familiar.

"I need you to find and hold Henders Cranston…"

"The historian?" she asked.

"Yes."

"But, Miss Imrial just went to see him…" she said

"I know, but you need to get there first. He's very dangerous and I suspect he's behind the attempts on my life."

"I'll try, but he's on the other side of the Island, at the Museum of Energy."

"Why would he…how quick can you get there?" Leo asked.

"I can call ahead to the guards at the museum…"

"Do that." Leo hung up.

"Do you know where the Museum of Energy is?"

"Yes, Sire, but there is no dock there."

"Fly directly to the museum," Leo said.

"That's not allowed, Sire…"

"That's an order," he tried.

"But Sire, it's not up to you. Only the Curator…" he started to explain.

"OK, let's try it another way. Is it allowed for you to fly over the museum?"

"Yes. We do it on tours all the time."

"Great. How low are you allowed to fly over it?" Leo asked.

"Well, when there are people present…"

"Never mind. Just fly over the museum." Leo gave in.

"Can do!"

When they reached the museum Leo asked the pilot to put the craft in hover mode. He was happy to do so. One of his two bodyguards spotted Imrial running up the stairs to the museum.

"Sire! There she is."

Leo ran to the window. He was right. She was pushing her way through the tourists. The crowds were small, but moving steadily in and out of the museum. Leo went back to the cockpit and sat in the co-pilot's seat.

"So, you can't land this in that bare patch over there?" Leo tried one last time.

"No, Sire."

"And I can't order you to?"

"No, Sire."

"But I can relieve you of duty?" Leo asked.

"Yes, Sire, of course, but…"

"You're fired," Leo said. It wasn't the term they used here, but the pilot understood what he meant.

The pilot let go of the controls.

"Yes, Sire." He gave Leo a smile.

"Hold on boys!" Leo yelled back to the guards.

It was a good thing the craft was made so well. Leo had watched carefully, but missed the way the pilot used the pedals to balance the ship. At first they leapt to the side. The guards, who had left their seats, were thrown against the windows.

"Sorry," Leo said.

Leo played the pedals, trying different combinations, one up, one down, both up, both down. The craft pitched and bounced.

Just before they hit the ground, the ship righted itself and they landed with a thud. The front legs had crushed a picnic table and one of the back ones was propped on a boulder. Leo looked over at the pilot and noticed his feet playing the pedals. If he hadn't helped, they would have landed upside down. As it was, they were seriously off balance. The two guards who had been tossed about ran over to the left side of the craft to keep it from tipping over. The other guards unbuckled and joined them.

"Sire, if you reinstate me, I can take the ship to the dock."

"Not yet," Leo said. "How do I open the doors?"

He pointed to a switch. Leo toggled it and the back doors opened.

"Do you have a portable communicator on board?"

He handed Leo a small clip-on device. Leo clipped it onto his shirt and half crawled, half climbed to the doors.

"You have to turn the dial to turn it on," the pilot called out to him.

When Leo got to the doors, he realized the engines were still running, and due to his poor job of landing, the jets were blowing dirt up into the back of the ship. He couldn't see. Just as he started to turn to go back, the engines cut off. Leo looked at the pilot.

"Oops," he said. Another smile.

Once the air settled, Leo looked out and saw he had to jump eight feet to the ground.

When he hit the ground, he saw a team of museum guards running over to the ship.

"Sire…we are to escort you."

Leo was surprised. He thought they would be coming to arrest him for landing the hopper on the lawn.

"I need that ship righted," Leo said as he ran past them toward the museum.

The lead guard barked out orders and then ran after him. Leo could hear him blowing a whistle to clear a path. Leo didn't have a whistle, so he shouted and pushed his way through the crowd. When the guard caught up, Leo found that the whistle worked a lot better.

When they entered the museum, they didn't have to ask directions. Another guard met them at the entrance.

"This way, Sire!" And off they went.

They ran up two flights of winding stairs. The stairs wrapped around the outside of the building, oddly shaped, like an old fashioned light bulb. When they reached the second floor landing, there was another guard. Leo felt like a baton in a relay race. They headed down a corridor, passing curious tourists the whole way.

"Have you arrested him?" Leo asked, nearly out of breath.

"No. Miss Imrial said to stay out of it."

Grrr. She could infuriate him so easily! How could she be so reckless?

And then it hit him…a sharp pricking in his belly. Leo gritted his teeth and pressed on.

They rounded one more bend and took a corridor to the left. As they approached a set of double doors Leo noticed two guards standing outside, weapons at the ready. He outran his escort and plowed through the doors.

He didn't like what he saw.

Imrial was lying at Henders' feet, her face covered with a white powder. It looked like flour, but Leo knew better. Whatever it was, it was stopping her from breathing. She was holding her throat, heaving, trying to catch her breath. But it wasn't working. Her neck and ears were actually turning blue.

Leo ran, without thinking, without hesitation, at Henders. The killer reached into his robe, but before he could pull his hand out, Leo ducked his head and launched himself, ramming his shoulder into Henders' stomach. Henders went flying back against the window. It cracked, but didn't break. They both ended up on the ground. Leo crawled over to Imrial and yelled out orders.

"Help me. Grab her hands and feet." She was thrashing even worse, her eyes showed were wide and wild - she couldn't get her lungs to work.

Two of the guards obeyed, while the other two went over to Henders Cranston. They grabbed at her hands and feet. She wasn't fighting them. She didn't even realize they were there. But her thrashing made it hard to get a hold of her.

"Stop it!" Leo yelled into her face. It got her attention enough to allow the guards to get her hands and feet. They put their weight forward onto her, holding her down.

Thank God for television! Leo took his meager

knowledge of first aid and added what he'd seen in countless TV shows.

He frantically brushed the powder away from her face. There was a little left so he blew forcefully at it.

Leo heard a commotion behind him – the guards trying to subdue Henders…but he couldn't take the time to look.

Leo pinched her nose shut, and covered her mouth with his. Leo breathed out air into her lungs. They filled. He turned his mouth away from her as a cloud of powder-filled-air expelled from her lips. He breathed in a deep gulp of clean air and reengaged her mouth. Leo forced more air into her lungs, and this time let go of her nose. A cloud of dust shot out of her nose like dragon's breath.

The commotion behind him stopped.

Leo repeated the process five more times before her exhalations were clear of the powder.

Her eyes calmed as the clean air finally reached her starving lungs.

She was breathing. Shallow at first, but steady.

Her eyes told him all he needed to hear - she was sorry, she was grateful, she was going to live.

"You can let go now," he said.

The guards let her hands and feet go. She didn't move, but her breathing was getting stronger.

Leo sat down next to her.

"Sire."

"Yes?" He remembered Henders, and the pain in his stomach.

"He's escaped."

"How?" Leo looked over to where the guards lay, sleeping heavily. They had blue powder around their faces. "Never mind. Take her back to the palace."

"But what about Henders Cranston? Shouldn't we go

after him?"

"No, take her back. Now." They picked her up and headed out of the room.

The lead guard stopped. "What about them?" he asked, pointing to the two sleeping guards.

"I think they'll be alright. Call a medic if you like. In fact, call your Captain and have her send a squad over here." Leo followed them to the door. As they passed the threshold, Leo stopped and closed the door, locking it.

"Sire?" Leo heard the lead guard call through the door.

"Call your Captain and be quick about it," Leo said as he wheeled about; the pin pricking in his stomach was constant now.

"You can't escape, not without going through me," Leo said to Henders. "And my guess is that your little invisibility powder, or whatever it is, won't last forever." Leo scanned the room in the same way he had seen Imrial do it, but he couldn't see Henders. His enemy was smart enough not to make a sound.

"It'll probably wear off before the Captain arrives with more guards," Leo said. He knew what Henders would have to do, it was the only way for him to escape, and Leo knew he'd have to do it soon. Henders remained silent.

"It's a shame you couldn't be king...but the Oracles don't select successors, they only tell what will happen. They can't be wrong," Leo said, trying to provoke a response. He remembered what the Second Elder had taught him, that if he truly believed in the Oracles, he wouldn't have to fear being killed. Then again, being injured, crippled, or paralyzed may not stop the prophecy – and would be a lousy end to the day.

"What? You think it's because I want to be king?"

Henders said from somewhere to Leo's right. His sudden break of silence made Leo jump slightly, although he had been sure he was still in the room. Leo wheeled around slowly to face where he thought the voice had come from.

"What else? Or is it just revenge?" Leo said calmly. Now that he had him talking, he didn't want to do anything to make him stop.

"Noooo!" Henders yelled as he attacked. Leo braced himself for impact, since he couldn't tell when he would hit him, but then Leo had an urge to duck. Leo dropped as low as he could. He felt Henders' knee hit his chest as his would-be killer went somersaulting over him. From the sound, Leo figured he slammed into the floor pretty hard.

It was quiet again for a few moments, and then Leo heard a moan.

"So, if not revenge, why do you want to kill me?" Leo asked.

"If I prove them fallible, then all bets are off! I can be king and bring my father out of exile!" he said from somewhere on Leo's left. It sounded like he was still on the floor. "I wanted to be king because that's what my father wanted! I didn't know he had to leave…but only the king can bring someone out of exile."

"Why not ask the King of Terence?" Leo asked, although he knew the answer. Leo needed to keep him talking until whatever was making him invisible wore off.

"I did. He refused." Leo could tell he was standing up now. Leo doubted he'd try running at him again. This time he would try a more subtle tactic.

"Why?"

"Because he feared losing the crown back to my father," he said. "Once I'm king, he'll be the one in exile." The voice was coming closer.

"If you really only wanted your father back, there must be another way," Leo said.

"I've read every law, every rule, and the history of my country...there is no other way." The voice was nearly in front of Leo. He couldn't risk losing focus.

Leo had to be prepared for the next attack. The wild, uncontrolled anger was gone from Henders' voice. He was back to being a calculating academic with a taste for murder. Leo had to stay ready.

He bent his knees a little and stared intently ahead.

Leo was ready for any attack Henders threw at him – but he wasn't ready for the door behind him to be burst open, slamming into his back and throwing him head first to the floor in the middle of the room.

The Captain of the guard and two burly security officers tumbled into the room. They had broken down the door without hesitation. Leo felt the breeze of Henders' robes pass by his face on the way out of the room. Leo grabbed for him, but missed.

"Stop him!" Leo yelled. The two other guards by the door were coming in with swords drawn. Leo was sure Henders had slipped by them.

"Who, Sire?" they said simultaneously.

The Captain and her human battering rams got to their feet. She came over to help Leo up while the guards searched the room. Leo slammed the side of his fist into the floor three times, growling out loud.

"No! You let him go!" he said. The Captain took a step back, but kept her offered hand out for him to grasp.

Leo took her hand and let her help him gain his feet.

"Where is Imrial?"

"She's at the dock, on your ship. She's being guarded." She looked him over, searching for wounds.

"I'm fine. Get me to the dock." He was still angry.

"I'm sorry, Sire."

"Put out an APB on Henders Cranston, he's the one who's been trying to kill me," Leo demanded.

"An ape bee?" She asked, even as she was raising her sleeve to her mouth to try and comply.

"An all-points-bulletin…just tell *everyone*."

"Yes, Sire."

"Oh, and let them know, he's invisible. At least for now. I don't know how long he'll be that way, though," Leo said.

"Sire?" She looked at him like he was crazy.

"Just do it, and get us back to Nahasar." Leo felt too exposed. Especially when his killer was invisible. Leo started out of the room. The two sword-wielding guards immediately fell in step with him – one in front, one behind.

Leo could hear the Captain ordering the two battering rams to help their sleeping compatriots, while also telling her sleeve that Henders Cranston should be arrested on *sight*. Leo almost laughed.

Talent - A sacred gift given to the common person, transforming him or her to a status of extraordinary. A gift that should be cherished and used; not wasted, not hidden, not ignored.

- Source Unknown

Talent - A curse, a blessed curse.

- Leo Hardy, King of Nahasar

15

Hours.

After all this time, Leo had only a few hours before he would be crowned King of Nahasar.

"I don't believe this will make any difference." Leo was trying to explain to the Elder Five, Grans, Imrial, Kanthor J. Noss, and Santore Noss that his coronation would not stop Henders Cranston.

"But…" Grans started.

"No. I understand his motivation. If the Oracles are proven wrong, he wins. As long as generations of Hardy-rule doesn't occur, he wins. I don't think he even cares if he gets caught – as long as I'm dead."

"But no rational…" started the Second Elder.

"He's not rational," Leo said. "The whole idea that killing me would solve his problems is irrational."

"Crazy is more like it," Santore Noss said.

"I don't know," Leo said.

"But it is possible," the Third Elder began, "if he made himself invisible by using the powder I suspect, and he wasn't already off balance, the drug could likely have pushed him over the edge."

"That would fit," the Fourth Elder said.

"So what do you recommend? That we cancel the

coronation?" It was the First Elder.

"No, that won't stop him either," Leo said decisively. He was in charge, and he found that he liked it. "We can't let our guard down after the ceremony. Until he's found…"

"Until he's stopped," Kanthor corrected.

"Stopped," Grans agreed. She was looking at Leo with the unspoken message that she knew he wasn't being totally forthright. Leo smiled at her, not to reassure her that everything was going to be alright, but that he would discuss it with her later.

"Until he's stopped, I won't be safe," Leo finished.

"Then we'll have to find him and stop him," Imrial said. She ushered the guards out, barking orders as she went.

The Elders and the two Noss' also left to give Leo a chance to rest. Leo fell into one of the large chairs.

"OK, now that they're gone, tell me what you're actually thinking!" Grans said with a little anger.

Leo held up his finger, signaling to wait.

Imrial came back into the room. She was not as spry as normal. The doctors said that the experience she had been through, almost dying by asphyxiation at Henders' hands, had drained her.

She wouldn't take a break though. Imrial was not only weak, she was upset. Maybe she was embarrassed. She had been bested by a historian. She had tried to capture Henders on her own, and failed.

Leo wasn't sure though. Something definitely had her upset, but he wasn't convinced it was Henders. She hadn't spoken a word to him since they returned to the palace. She stubbornly took up a position behind his chair.

"Imrial, sit down." Leo pointed to the chair opposite his.

She started to argue. He could almost hear the tension in her, the readiness to fight. But she was too tired and weak.

She did as he asked. She sat in the chair and closed her eyes.

Leo needed some rest himself.

"So, what is it?" Grans asked, "I know you don't lie, but you obviously didn't share everything."

The adrenaline had worn off. He was actually exhausted. He closed his eyes. He spoke slowly and softly. It took effort to stay awake.

"The coronation. I need you both to be at your best at the ceremony."

Imrial's eyes opened and she looked at him.

"He'll try during the ceremony," Leo said.

"What? That would be crazy," Grans argued. She was the only one with any energy.

Imrial sat watching, quiet.

"No, it's quite logical. If I die in front of everyone, he will have proven quite publicly that the oracles can be wrong."

"Then we have to cancel the…" Grans started to stand up.

"No," Imrial whispered.

"I have to…" he started.

"I agree," she said. "You have to. And we have to catch him." She leaned back in the chair. Grans walked over to her and put a pillow beside her head. Imrial leaned against the pillow.

"Never mind that," Leo said as he got up, finally getting his second wind. He walked over to Imrial and scooped her up in his arms and carried her into the master bedroom. Grans followed. Leo waited for Grans to pull down the covers and he laid Imrial carefully on the bed. Grans covered her up while he headed back toward the main room. Leo could hear Grans singing a chorus of a song, softly as she closed the curtains, blocking out the setting sun.

Leo waited for her by the door. Imrial was beautiful. Obstinate and impulsive – but beautiful.

"She'll be out for a while," Grans said as she pushed him out of the doorway, closing the door behind her. "So, what's your plan?"

"Good question," Leo said. They had a little over five hours to come up with an answer.

All five nations were represented. The Great Hall was full. Now Leo understood why there was no furniture in the hall. There wasn't any room. It was packed tight, standing room only. He didn't know most of the people, but he was sure that he would be expected to meet every one of them after the coronation.

And they kept coming.

Leo was sure the hall was full, but more people kept coming in.

He had to wait until everyone was in place before he made his official entrance. He watched everything from a hidden balcony above the entrance to the hall. It was actually very exciting. It would have been exciting even without the possibility of another attempt on his life.

Leo had asked that all of the servants be invited, so the hall was full of those of noble birth and those of noble profession. Even young Philip attended. At least that peppered the crowd with some familiar faces.

Santore Noss introduced each guest as they arrived, so Leo made him introduce each servant as they came out of the kitchen, the hall, and the waiting rooms. Santore Noss wasn't happy about it, but he did an excellent job. Leo was surprised, and proud, that Santore announced each worker with the same pomp and circumstance as he did the royal and the powerful.

The Elder Five were in full, splendid dress.

Leo finally got to see the five Oracles. They seemed as unbelievably young as the Elders seemed old. He figured them to be about 5 years old each, if that. They were on the dais in front of the Elder Five. A straight path through the center of the hall was roped off with mobile poles that reminded him of the roped lines at an airport, bank or museum. Leo thought the walk down that aisle would look like a wedding march – Imrial would say it was more like a death march. Way too close to any possible assassins.

A different representative for the Curator was present...Leo thought his name was Michael. Interesting fellow. He was the first person Leo had seen on Elonce that actually seemed comfortable carrying one of those swords. He stood on the other side of the dais, opposite the Elder Five and the Oracles. In front of him was the official party: Kanthor J. Noss, Santore Noss, and of course Grans - Genevieve De Scioncia Hardy. She looked magnificent, happy, worried, and proud, all at the same time.

But the person Leo was looking for was nowhere to be seen. He knew Henders Cranston wouldn't let this opportunity pass. He had proven to be in a dangerous state of denial. Leo knew he didn't believe he could be stopped – he didn't believe he could be captured and tried for attempts on Leo's life. He was delusional. As with most fanatics, he had a single driving vision which could not be changed by logic or common sense. He only had one goal in mind, one possible result. He didn't see any consequences of his actions except his desired end. Leo finally understood the saying about genius and insanity being only a breath away from each other.

"Is everything ready?" Leo asked Imrial, who seemed more responsive after sleeping for three hours. She stood slightly behind him on his left side.

"Yes. I'm not sure why you think it'll work, but everything is ready," she said. She was fully engaged with her job as bodyguard to the future king. There would be no smiles until after the ceremony.

Leo gave her a smile anyway. "We'll have to wait and see."

Leo made one last check of his robes in the mirror and headed out of the room, to make his entrance.

Imrial maintained her place to his left while two guards joined, in-step, behind, and two in front. As they descended the stairs to the main floor, two more guards greeted them with a salute. They stepped out into the foyer and headed for the long walk. At each of the metal posts holding the ropes, there was another guard with his sword drawn in a ceremonial salute. At least, that's the reason Leo was given for their drawn weapons. He heard trumpet-like instruments sound a loud introduction. All heads in the room turned toward him.

Leo was a little awe-struck. He had been so focused on catching Henders that he hadn't really noticed the enormity of the occasion. Leo Hardy was not only on center stage, he was about to be crowned king!

The walk up the aisle must have taken forever - but Leo barely remembered it. He knew there were cheers, exhortations, and at least one shout of, "I love you Leo," but it was all a blur. He was sure the raucousness of the crowd was unusual for such an official occasion, but he was glad for it.

By the time Leo made it to the dais, the noise had abated and the seriousness of crowning a new king took over.

The ceremony was long. Leo made it worse (for

himself) by not enjoying the moment as much as he should have, at least at the beginning. He kept scanning the crowd for Henders. A third of the way through the ceremony, he resigned himself to the fact that Henders may not be in the crowd, that he could have been wrong. In fact, Leo didn't think he'd be able to move if he were in the crowd - invisible or not! It was definitely standing room only. After Leo had made it to the stage, the ropes were removed and even more people were allowed in. It looked like the Red Sea closing back in on the path God made for the escaping slaves in "The Ten Commandments" movie. Now it was so tight, no one could move.

When Leo realized the threat couldn't come from the crowd, he relaxed a little. The good part was that he finally started paying attention to the ceremony. It was a pretty neat event. Lots of dignitaries said nice things about his grandfather. Scrolls were read. The best part was when the Elder Five told stories explaining the history of Nahasar. With all of the advanced (compared to Earth) technology, they still preferred to convey history through storytelling. Leo loved it. If there was ever a profession he'd want to study for, storyteller would be it.

When it came time, Kanthor J. Noss was very excited to crown the new king. He gave a short, but spirited speech before he called for the crown and scepter of Nahasar.

"Ladies and gentlemen, it is with great honor that I relinquish the temporary hold I've had on the leadership of our great nation, Nahasar!" Applause and cheers filled the hall again. "As predicted by the Oracles, affirmed by the Elder Five, and blessed by the Curator – Leo Hardy is now to become the King of Nahasar. May his rule, and Nahasar's fortunes, travel along the one path to success."

At this, as coached, Leo rose and walked over to the empty throne. It wasn't much bigger than the chairs they were all using, but it was more ornate. It had gold and silver inlays throughout with colored gems at every joint. The cushions on the back, seat, and arms were a deep red velvet. When Leo sat on the chair another round of applause resounded. It was surprisingly comfortable.

Kanthor handed the crown to the Elder Five and the scepter to Grans. Grans handed Leo the scepter while the Elders placed the crown on his head, each holding it by one of the five points.

Santore Noss then took the podium.

"I present to you the new King of Nahasar, Leo Hardy." It was the fewest words Leo had ever heard come out of his mouth.

They all stayed in that pose - the Elder Five placing the crown, Grans handing Leo the scepter, for what seemed like ten minutes. Pictures were taken, cheers were yelled, and the applause seemed endless. After what must have been more like thirty seconds in reality, the Elder Five went back to their seats with Grans.

Leo approached the podium to make his acceptance speech. It would be his first public act as the King of Nahasar.

What a strange turn his life's journey had taken.

"Thank you." Another cheer rose from the crowd. Leo waited until it died down to continue. When it did, he smiled, and that made them cheer again, louder. Leo realized that the first cheer was perfunctory, but now they were cheering because he was smiling. Leo guessed it was a more honest response than they were used to. Leo had been coached on maintaining a kingly stature and aloofness – but he wasn't very good at it.

"Thank you," he tried again. This time the cheers

were a little less loud and lasted a shorter time.

"Thank you, I am very proud to be given the honor of ruling this country," Leo paused for effect – as Grans had coached him, "...our country, of Nahasar!" Cheers again. Again Leo smiled, and again the cheers got louder.

"I plan..." Again he had to wait.

"I plan to always make you proud of me, to..." Again cheering drowned him out.

"I plan to always make you proud of me, to be an instrument," pause, "...*your* instrument of peace, love, and mercy!" This got the results Grans had anticipated. The crowd went wild. They started chanting his name, "Leo, Leo, Leo." He could feel his face turning red. Leo smiled broadly and lowered his head in a sign of humility. He hadn't planned his reaction – but it had a great effect. What *he* had envisioned as a weakness, as a fault in his leadership - they viewed as a strength. Leo had worried that he wouldn't be able to lead because he didn't know the customs, or the rules of leadership. They, the people he was now responsible for, the people he was expected to lead, saw his 'roughness' as refreshing. Leo tried to speak, and found that he couldn't. His throat had tightened up with emotion. His eyes began to water.

Grans came to his rescue. She handed him a handkerchief and a glass of water. Leo wiped his eyes and took two sips of water. He handed them back to her and nodded. He didn't bother thanking her, as she wouldn't have been able to hear him over the cheering anyway.

Finally they settled down. Leo cleared his throat.

He decided to make his very first proclamation.

"As the King of Nahasar, with the approval of the leaders of the other four nations and the Elder Five, I hereby rescind the exile of William the Good, former King of Terence."

Everyone looked surprised, except the Second Elder. He just nodded and smiled.

No cheering. Not at first. The crowd seemed to be thinking it over. Word was out that the person behind the assassination attempts was the son of William the Good. For the most part, a concerted anger toward Henders Cranston and his family had permeated the land. That anger was why Henders couldn't afford to be recognized, but at the same time, that anger coupled with his increasing lack of stability was why Leo was sure he would attack again, here.

One by one, the leaders of the other four nations bowed in agreement. The King of Terrence was the first to bow, then the Elders, one by one, bowed in agreement. This Leo half expected, and fully hoped for, but then the rest of the official party on stage bowed. Both Noss', Grans, everyone.

A murmur started in the crowd. A low chant by someone.

"He is to be returned to his home where he will take care of his son, Henders Cranston, until such a time as he can stand trial for his crimes. That is, when he is captured."

The chant spread and gained strength. Finally it was loud enough that Leo could make it out.

"Leo the Merciful, Leo the Merciful, Leo the Merciful" filled the hall. Clapping rose up in accompaniment.

"Liar!" Leo heard from behind him. Or he thought he heard it. The shouting in the crowd wasn't as loud as the cheering had been before, but he still didn't believe he could hear any one voice.

What he heard was Henders' voice, a guttural, angry bark in his ear.

Leo swung around instinctively and immediately fell

to one knee. The pain in his stomach was a sharp stabbing pain. He could actually feel the air displaced above his head as something swung above him. Leo couldn't see his assailant. He couldn't hear anything but the crowd which was now cheering wildly. Later, Grans told him the crowd thought he had turned to bow to the official party - a very humble act for a king.

"Liar!"

Leo dove to his left and rolled. He could feel a thud on the ground beside him, where he had been a moment before. He could see the floor of the podium split open in a fine crack.

Grans told him later that his humility seemed to be followed by exuberant celebration, a wild, frenetic type of dance.

Leo wished he could hear better...but the pain in his stomach died down to a mild thrum. He guessed what had happened and dove at the space in front of where he had been. Leo lowered his head and led with his right shoulder, his arms out in front of him to grab Henders.

His guess was right. Whatever weapon Henders was using was stuck in the floor and he was trying to pull it out when Leo tackled him.

Imrial jumped forward, realizing what was happening. Unfortunately, she tripped over the weapon embedded in the floor, and went sprawling over the dais into the crowd, which had burst through the ring of guards and was standing, cheering at the edge of the stage. They were screaming like schoolgirls at a Beatles concert. When Imrial fell into their midst they caught her and started passing her through the crowd. They held her above their heads, and Leo couldn't help thinking his coronation had become a rock concert! Leo could see her out of the corner of his eye, and she was desperately trying to get them to stop passing her around like a beach ball, to no avail.

Leo felt a spatter of spittle hit his face.

Leo had Henders beneath him, but it was very difficult to subdue what he couldn't see.

His stomach went back to serious stabbing pain conditions.

Leo lowered his head, putting his forehead onto what he figured to be Henders' chest. The blow swung at his chin hit the back of his head instead. Henders let out a groan of pain. Leo reached out to where he figured Henders' arms would be and caught one of them. He felt another stab and swung his face to the other side of Henders' chest. The blow hit the back of his head again. This time it hurt Leo a little, but not as much as Henders.

The group on the dais was slow to come around to what was happening. They thought, like the crowd, that Leo was doing some kind of jig. When Imrial went sailing into the crowd, they were caught up with watching her. When they brought their attention back to Leo, he seemed to be floating off the floor a few inches, swinging his head back and forth.

Leo still couldn't hear much, due to the crowd. They had begun singing the national anthem of Nahasar. A decidedly more upbeat, danceable tune than he would have expected. Most anthems he'd ever heard were slow and dull. Not this one.

Henders grabbed the back of Leo's robes and they started tumbling over, back and forth. It looked like Leo was rolling around on the floor. His crown fell off and rolled over to Santore Noss, who picked it up and joined in the singing of the anthem. Everyone on the dais was now singing.

Grans finally figured it out, but no one could hear her yelling for help.

The two wrestlers stopped rolling again, this time

with Henders on top. Leo lost his grip on Henders' right arm and his stomach tightened in a knot. Leo just hoped Henders was still trying to hit him in the face. He shifted his head to the right. Henders' fist slammed into the floor beside his ear.

Leo could hear Henders' yell of pain over the crowd. Henders jerked back violently, tearing out of Leo's grasp altogether. He jumped off of Leo.

Leo waited for a second, checking his warning system. No pin-prick, no stabs. The danger for the moment had passed.

Leo stood up, and looked over at Grans. She looked very worried. Everyone else on the dais started clapping. They figured he had finished his dance. Leo looked out into the crowd and saw Imrial near the rear. The crowd let her down, but she wasn't going to make it back to the dais any time soon.

Leo felt another painful shot to his stomach – this was the worst yet. Like when Gramps was killed.

He looked at Imrial, but she was at the back of the crowd now, and he couldn't see if she was in danger. Leo wheeled around and looked at Grans. She was standing up, leaning back. Leaning back in an odd way. It didn't seem right. He noticed she was holding her chin very high, and her arms were stiff at her sides.

Then Leo noticed the thin line of blood across her neck.

Leo walked slowly toward her.

Everyone on the dais bowed as he approached.

Grans began walking backward. She carefully walked down the back steps of the platform.

Leo followed.

Grans walked backward into the North hall, past the guards who were also singing. They bowed when Leo approached. She backed into an open room. It was the reception room.

Leo followed.

Henders pulled her around the doorway, allowing Leo to enter the room. After he was inside, Henders kicked the door closed.

Leo's ears were ringing, but at least he could hear, the noise of the crowd was muffled in the room.

"Let her go," he said with much more calmness than he felt.

"Of course," Henders said, equally calm. He pushed Genevieve to the side, surprisingly gently, as if not wanting to hurt her. She stumbled a little but righted herself before she could fall. She leaned on a table of pastries.

Henders obviously didn't know that Grans was an agent in her time. She immediately grabbed two pies and launched them one after the other where she thought he was. He never saw it coming.

"It's you I want…" he began, before the first pie hit him in the right shoulder, splattering crème and filling across his back and neck. The second pie hit him in the side of his head, covering his face. He sputtered, spitting the pie out of his mouth.

Leo didn't hesitate. Henders still had a knife, and although he was now partly visible, he had a great advantage. Leo would have preferred to strike his arm and make him lose the weapon, but he went for what he could see.

And then luck smiled on Leo.

Henders had the knife in his right hand, and he chose to use the back of that hand to wipe the filling from his eyes. Leo could tell by the way he wiped at the goo.

Leo charged hard. He hit Henders in the chest with his shoulder and grabbed at the hand holding the knife as they slammed into the door. He got his wrist and without pause, twisted hard. Henders let out a cry of pain and the knife clattered on the floor, still invisible. Leo expected a blow from behind as his back was to Henders now, but all Henders was interested in was getting his aching wrist out of Leo's grip. He pulled hard, while shoving Leo with his left hand.

Leo stumbled forward.

"No! This is not right!" Henders yelled as he ran toward a different table. When Leo turned, he could see his partially pie covered form at another table, frantically wiping his face clean with a large cloth napkin.

"Get help," Leo told Grans, who was standing with two more pastry weapons in her hands. She dropped them on the floor and slipped out the door.

"Henders, I didn't lie," Leo said as he approached him.

Leo knew he could take him easily now that he was disarmed. Henders wasn't much of a fighter.

"My father is dead! He's dead!" He stopped wiping his face and seemed to be bent over. Leo could still make out his right shoulder and part of his head. He hadn't cleaned off any from his back either.

"No, he's here, in the castle. I'll take you to him if you want," Leo said, closing the gap. Leo planned to spin him around and bear hug him until the guards arrived.

"He's dead," he said very softly. "You killed him."

Leo felt sorry for him. He was losing his mind.

And then Leo felt it – the sharpest pain he had ever felt shot into his stomach. At first Leo thought he had been actually stabbed with a knife, but the pain started inside. It was his warning system and it was screaming at him.

Leo heard the cloak's rustle, and Henders straightened up.

He took a deductive guess – a guess that if he was wrong, might cost him his life. Leo took in a deep breath and held it. The pain in his stomach grew – if that was possible. He had to ignore it. He had to stay still, be an easy target. He stood listening, holding his breath.

"I'm sorry," Henders said, directly in front of Leo. Leo could hear him start to inhale deeply.

Leo waited until the sound of him inhaling stopped and before Henders could, Leo blew out all of the air he was holding in his lungs as forcefully as he could at what he hoped was Henders' face.

Leo had guessed right.

Henders had a handful of powder ready to use against him, but Leo beat him to it. The powder shot off of Henders' hand into his face. As soon as Leo exhaled he dove to his right and rolled away.

Henders blinked twice and exhaled, shooting the swirling powder in front of, and on his face, into a small cloud. Leo could see the red dust swirling, and then settling toward the ground. Leo got into a crouch and waited for it to clear.

Once the powder cleared, Leo walked over to Henders. He could see specks of red powder floating in the air in the shape of Henders' face. Henders didn't move or make a sound.

The first guard came through the door with his sword drawn.

"Sire, are you alright?"

"Yes, I believe I am," Leo said. "Get a doctor."

Grans came through the door with Imrial as the guard left. Two more guards came in.

Imrial looked around, and figured it all out quickly. She smiled approvingly at him.

Grans came over and held his arm. "Are you alright?"

"Yes, I'm fine. I want him taken care of."

"Of course," Imrial said with a grin. It looked a little wicked to Leo. He resolved once again never to get on her bad side.

"No, I mean cared for." She looked at Leo like *he* was crazy. His face tightened, and he said as sternly as possible. "I don't want his father seeing him this way."

"Yes, Sire," she said.

Leo had to look at her to see if she was mocking him, but she wasn't. She was looking at him strangely though. She had never looked at him that way. He wished he could read faces like Grans so he could figure out what she was thinking.

"We'll be at the reception line. See if you can have this cleaned up before the guests get here," Leo said less harshly.

"Yes, Sire, I'll see to it myself," she said, and then she smiled. Not the smile she used when he made her laugh or the smile that meant that she found his ways funny. This was a new smile.

So, he took the second biggest risk of his life. He took two steps to her, and kissed her quickly on the mouth. She closed her lips long enough, and quick enough, so he didn't kiss her teeth, and then the same smile returned.

Imrial followed through with her normal level of perfection. Henders was carried out to a private room and once the invisibility wore off, was washed and dressed in more stately clothes. The doctor and the Third Elder determined that the powders Henders used had indeed poisoned him, and drove him insane. Henders' studies of Alchemy stopped short of the reasons the powders were banned - they were extremely toxic.

The doctor believed that once the poisons worked their way out of his system, he might fully recover.

Leo hadn't lied of course. A simple change of the laws of Terrence allowed William the Good to return from exile without a right to reclaim the throne. After that, it was a simple matter to get the approval of the King of Terrence, and everyone else. Henders' father asked for, and was granted permission to take Henders back into exile with him. It turned out that the relaxing life of an exile was just what the Cranstons needed. The Second Elder accompanied them to ensure that they settled in and that Henders fully recovered. When Leo asked him why he was going, he kept muttering something about a fortune cookie and needing a vacation.

Although Leo thought Imrial was over her embarrassment, Grans assured him she was still angry. And worse, he was starting to feel she was angry with him, not with herself. Leo wasn't sure what to do about her. By the time she returned from her assignment with Henders, the coronation was over. The hall had been emptied and cleaned. It took all evening. Leo escorted Grans back to her suite and wished her a good night. He knew he had to talk to Imrial. He had to find out why she was so angry, and he had to talk to her about her future.

The truth was that Leo didn't want her to leave. He had become very accustomed to her presence.

He saw one of the Elder Five. "Fourth Elder?"

"I'm the First Elder. How can I help you, King Leo?"

"I was looking for Miss Imrial" Leo said after a short hesitation.

"She's not back from the island, but I suspect she'll be back in the morning." He said smiling.

Leo wondered if he was that obvious.

"Thanks," Leo said. His talk with Imrial would have to wait.

The next morning, Leo was awakened by Santore Noss. A loud rapping at the door jolted Leo from his sleep. When he opened the door, Santore started in immediately with another speech. Leo had realized that Santore rarely had a conversation. Just speeches.

"The new and merciful King Leo, by request of..." he began.

Leo expected it to be a summons by the Elder Five, or the rulers of the other four nations, or even the Curator.

"...Sire, your presence is requested by..." Santore was having serious trouble getting this speech out. Leo had never seen him have this problem before.

"Spit it out," Leo encouraged.

Instead of giving him the confidence to finish, Santore Noss stopped cold and looked puzzled.

"I mean, just say what you have to say," Leo corrected himself.

"Yes sire, of course," but he didn't continue.

"Did someone want to see me?" Leo tried again.

"Yes. Yes, that's it. The cooks, the housekeepers, the groundskeepers, well, the staff."

"What about the staff?" Leo asked.

"They'd like to have an audience with you." He seemed satisfied that he finally got it out.

"I'll be down in half an hour."

Santore bowed and closed the door. Leo needed to shower.

When he made his way downstairs to the hall he found the entire staff gathered and waiting for him. Santore was to have a second chance at making a speech. He stood on the dais with a microphone.

"Sire, if you would please come forward?" Leo could

tell this was not normal.

He worked his way through the staff who were silently watching. When he made it to the dais he climbed the steps and stood next to Santore Noss. He wondered where Grans and Imrial were.

"Sire, the staff has asked me to read a proclamation which they want put into the official historical records of Nahasar." Now Leo knew this was irregular. He looked around and finally found what he expected to see. Imrial, Grans, and Kanthor were all at the back of the hall in the secret balcony room, watching. They didn't bother to hide behind the curtains. Leo could plainly make them out.

"Then read the proclamation."

"The staff of the House of Nahasar wish to proclaim through official channels, to be recorded in the official history of the country of Nahasar, the following as a statement from the workers to the new King of Nahasar, Leo the Merciful, Leo the Honest, Leo the Brave," he paused for effect.

"To the rightful ruler of Nahasar, 'thank you.'"

They all stood watching and waiting to see what Leo would say or do. Some creative ideas ran through his mind, along with a really good joke he had heard from his science teacher last year...but nothing seemed appropriate or worthy. He was truly humbled - and he didn't know how to show it. He approached the microphone and said what came to him without thinking.

"You're very welcome."

The applause came. Leo turned to Santore, who immediately bowed. Leo returned his bow and then held out his hand. Santore Noss hesitated only for a moment and then took it with the biggest grin on his face Leo had ever seen. When he was able to wrench his hand free,

Leo turned and bowed to the staff. They all bowed back and started cheering. Leo walked down the steps and spent the next hour shaking every staff members' hand. He learned later that it was the first time they had ever touched a ruler although some had been serving the House of Nahasar their whole lives.

When Leo finally made it to the end of the hall, Young Philip was waiting. Leo held out his hand and instead of taking it, Young Philip bowed. Leo returned the bow and put out his hand again. He took it, laughed, and pulled Leo to him for a hug. The giant pushed Leo away to arm's length and said, "Leonard would be proud of you." Then he turned and left quickly, pulling a handkerchief from his back pocket.

Grans, Kanthor J. Noss, and Imrial came into the hall.

"Nicely done Leo," Grans said as she kissed his cheek.

Kanthor bowed and then shook his hand. Leo was glad he was wrong about him.

Imrial bowed perfunctorily and shook his hand stiffly.

"Do you still work for me?" Leo asked her.

"If you say I do," she answered.

"Good. I need your help. Let's walk." He led her out of the hall and out into the rear grounds. They walked through the garden to what looked like a playing field of some kind. Neither spoke. She walked on his left, one stride behind him. He knew this was the official position she was supposed to take so he didn't complain.

"Where's the lake?" Leo asked. He had seen it from the air and from the castle, but he wasn't finding it on the ground.

"To your left about a hundred yards."

They continued their walk in silence. When they reached the lake Leo easily found the dock. It was too early for the staff's children to be swimming and too late for the guys he had seen fishing from his window when dawn crept across the castle grounds. The lake was theirs. Leo walked out to the end of the small dock. He had seen kids jumping off of it into the water, and had seen the small boats tethered to it. He knew this was a good place to find privacy.

Leo sat on the edge of the platform. He took off his shoes and socks and lowered his feet into the cold water. Imrial stood to his left and slightly behind him.

"Take off your shoes and join me."

"I prefer to stand," she tried.

"I understand," he said. She put on a smug smile. It wasn't really a smile, or at least he really couldn't see it. But he knew she was smiling on the inside.

"But, since you work for me, sit down, take off your shoes, and put your feet in the water." Leo could get to like giving orders.

She did as ordered. Once her feet were in the water Leo laid back and put his hands under his head. He looked up at the beautiful blue morning sky of Nahasar. He was truly home.

Leo waited.

Finally she laid back and looked up at the sky.

"So, what's wrong? I thought you were upset because Cranston had bested you, but I don't think you're full of that much pride."

Leo knew it would be easier for her to talk without having to look at him.

"Nothing's wrong."

Maybe it wouldn't be easier. He had been wrong before.

"I know you don't have to tell the truth, but I'm getting used to the way you lie. Isn't it against the law or something for you to lie to the king?"

She repressed a laugh. "No, there's no such rule."

"Fine. Maybe we should see about creating one. In

any case, I think you owe me the truth."

"I guess you're right," she said. And then she stayed there, looking at the sky, silent.

Leo waited for her to be ready to tell him.

He watched more than a few clouds float by.

"The guards told me what you did," she finally offered.

This was way too open-ended for him to reply. He had done a lot since he arrived on Elonce. Nothing that he was ashamed of and nothing that he thought would make her angry. So, he waited again.

"When Cranston knocked me out with his stupid powder. They told me what you did."

Leo thought back to the event. He remembered tackling Henders, he remembered sending the guards with Imrial back to the ship while he tried to capture him, he remembered saving Imrial's life. There was a lot that happened. He still didn't know what had made her angry. Perhaps it was how he locked himself in a room with his assassin.

While he waited for her to give him more, he analyzed what she had said. She had said 'knocked me out' - not 'tried to kill me.'"

An idea was coming to him.

"You kissed me," she said.

He laughed out loud. He sat up and laughed some more. She sat up next to him, her face growing red with anger. He knew he should stop, he knew she had a temper, but he couldn't help it.

"You kissed me - a lot! That was very improper!" She yelled in a loud whisper. She wanted to shout at him, but she also didn't want anyone to hear.

The dock and the lake may have been deserted but voices carried across still waters.

Leo laughed harder.

She started punching him in his arm. Leo thought she'd keep hitting him until he stopped laughing, so he worked harder to gain control of himself.

"Okay, okay," he pleaded through his giggles. "I'm sorry."

"As well you should be!" She said, misunderstanding.

It made Leo start laughing again. She gave him a really good punch in his shoulder.

"I'm sorry I can't stop laughing," he said, and she pouted. She looked so cute pouting over being taken advantage of that he stopped laughing.

"I wasn't kissing you," Leo explained.

"The guards said…" then he could see her thinking it through - she knew he couldn't lie. "So what were you...?"

"I was saving your life. You couldn't breathe with the powder in your lungs so I helped you clear it out." Leo really did feel bad about laughing at her. She was very serious about the whole thing. She was embarrassed first because Cranston had bested her and then, she was told that he had been kissing her when she was incapacitated.

"Trust me, I wouldn't have kissed you," he said, adding too much.

"Really? Why not?"

"I meant, I would have gladly, no I meant…" Leo stumbled over himself. She stood up, angry again - a different kind of angry though.

Leo stood up to stop her from leaving.

"So, you wouldn't kiss me? What was the thing you did yesterday? When you stumbled over yourself almost knocking me over?" She exaggerated.

"That was different."

"Why? Was that a peck on the lips between friends?" She turned and took two steps away.

"No! I wanted to kiss you then."

She wheeled on him. "But not before?"

"No. Not when you were dying and the maniac trying to kill us was still in the room. I was saving your life."

"But yesterday you wanted to kiss me."

"Yes," he snapped back.

"And today?" she asked.

Leo closed the distance between them and moved in for a real kiss. Not the, 'peck that barely missed her teeth yesterday,' kiss. But a real kiss. The kind of kiss he really wanted to give her.

He was wrong again.

Before he could wrap his arms around her, she expertly shoved him hard in the chest with both hands shifting her weight forward. He went flying off the edge of the dock into the cold water with a sizable splash. When he came up, she was finishing putting on her shoes. Leo climbed up the ladder, shivering from the drenching.

She leaned over the edge and grabbed the back of his head. She lowered her lips to his and kissed him.

It was the best kiss he ever had.

When she pulled away, she smiled. He knew it wasn't possible, but time seemed to stand still. The water was no longer cold, the wind no longer blew, and the birds stopped singing. Everything froze in time. He was halfway out of the water, on the ladder, looking up at the most beautiful woman he had ever seen. She was always pretty, but at that moment, she held his heart in her hands. When time finally started up again, he smiled.

"Thanks," she said.

"For what?"

But she didn't answer. She just walked off.

Leo kept smiling all the way back to the castle.

I know now what it means to be born again. To experience a rebirth. Until we find love, our heart doesn't truly beat, our minds do not truly think, and our souls do not truly sing.

- Leo Hardy, King of Nahasar

16

Thanks for listening to my story. I would have asked one of the excellent historians on Elonce to capture this story, but Grans convinced me it was my story to tell. I apologize for how poorly it was written, but I know Grans was right. I had to be the one to tell it. You may be curious about how things ended up.

I pardoned Sean Bulthoware after Imrial confirmed his story. He turned out to be a better musician than mechanic so I arranged for him to attend music school on a scholarship. Young Philip was his sponsor.

I made Young Philip my lead counsel.

Kanthor J. Noss retained his position as Head of the Senate.

Santore Noss left his post to become an orator at the Island of Museums. His job required him to make speeches, on the hour, six hours a day, five days a week.

I fired Grans as my counselor. It may seem selfish, but I wanted her to be my grandmother, nothing more. I needed family more than I needed counselors. Of course, the world had other plans for her. She eventually took on a special assignment for the Curator.

I made Imrial the chief of security for the entire nation - a new post I created. She complained about being away from the action and becoming a bureaucrat, but she accepted the position. She said she'd do the job until she was sure the nation's security was well taken care of - and then she'd turn it over to someone else. I thought the job would give us time together, but as it turned out, shortly after her acceptance of the position, Imrial had a time warp adventure of her own. Even after living through my own unbelievable story, I wouldn't have believed what happened. I wouldn't have believed it except I witnessed a lot of it with my own eyes. But, that's not my story to tell.

I learned a lot in the years that followed.

I learned that I could forgive even the most heinous crimes, although I still had to give out punishments.

I learned that ruling wasn't easy, and my grandmother was still wiser than I.

I learned that although I was miles, years, and maybe universes away from my birthplace, I was now home.

But the most important thing I learned was that a smile meant the same thing here as back on Earth, and it was all the reward I ever needed.

Since this story involves time (and place) travel, it's hard to be sure if this is the end or the beginning, or sometime in the middle. But, this *is* the end of this book. Thanks for spending time with us.

Made in the USA
Las Vegas, NV
22 February 2022

44379841R00125